FAMILIAR PROTOCOL

WITCHIN' IMPOSSIBLE COZY MYSTERIES
BOOK 3

RENEE GEORGE

BARKSIDE OF THE MOON PRESS

Familiar Protocol: Witchin' Impossible Cozy Mysteries Book 3

2nd Edition

Copyright © 2018 by Renee George

Publisher: Barkside of the Moon Press

Print ISBN: 978-1-947177-27-7

For my sister Robbin.
You are a rock star!!

ACKNOWLEDGMENTS

A special THANK YOU to the fabulous Robyn Peterman, an awesomely funny writer and my favorite cookie, for allowing me the privilege to write in her world and then turning around and letting me have it back to do with what I please! I love your guts, woman!!

Also, I must thank the usual suspects, my BFF sister and most fabulous beta reader Robbin. Thank you for all the brainstorming and staying up with me late at night.

To my Rebels, you all RAWK! I love you like I love my leg.

To my fans, I would not be anything without you. Seriously. If you keep reading, I'll keep writing! Thank you. Thank you. Thank you. If I were reviewing you all, you would get five-gazillion stars and a million-gazillion smooches.

Oh! And, as always, black coffee. Without you, I couldn't get out of bed in the afternoon, let alone write a single word.

A disgruntled bear fiancé. A wanted familiar. A hairless cat named Lonnie. For Hazel Kinsey, it's just another day in Paradise Falls.

When Hazel's familiar Tizzy the Squirrel fell in love with another familiar, they had no idea her furry pal would gain witch magic.

Apparently, that's a big no-no for the High Familiar Clowder, the council who rules all familiars. When the Clowder shows up in Paradise Falls to decommission Tizzy and send her to the in-between, Haze defies the stick-in-the-butt jerkfaces by refusing to trade in Tiz for a new familiar.

But the Clowder means business. They strip Hazel of her magic, leaving her no better than a human. Worst of all, she's lost the mating scent she shared with her bear-beau, the hunky-handsome Ford Baylor. Without it or her witch powers, she can never be a real mate for him.

With only seventy-two hours to find a solution to her familiar and fiancé problems, Hazel and pals must find a way to stop the Clowder, get Hazel witchified again, save Tizzy and her true love, and oh yeah, battle sinister forces intent on glomming as much power as possible.

Yep. Just another day in Paradise Falls.

CHAPTER 1

"Oh, my goddess! If there's a witch heaven, this must be what it tastes like." My eyes rolled back as the sweet confection of lemon buttercream and raspberry filling between the six layers of moist vanilla sponge, lit up my taste buds like cheap Roman candles on the Fourth of July.

Tizzy, my flying squirrel familiar, and I had been trying different flavors of cake since three o'clock. It was now four-fifteen. Luckily, one of the perks of being a witch was not gaining weight, which is a good thing, considering I'd easily put away twenty-million-bazillion calories. All sugar and fat. *Mmmm mmmm mmm.* I couldn't think of a better way to spend a Sunday afternoon.

"Doorknobs and broomsticks, Haze. Do I need to book a room so you can be alone with the cake?" Tiz said. She dragged her tiny clawed finger through the frosting and put it to her lips. Her big brown eyes brightened as she took another swipe. "I'll make that a room for three. Wow. That is orgasmic."

"Uh-huh," I mumbled through my fifth bite. Then I realized what she'd said. "Ew. I do not want to think about you and…" I waved my hand at her.

"And orgasms?" Tizzy tried a little chunk of the sponge. "Yum." Her long dark brown eyelashes fluttered as she savored the moment. After, she opened her eyes and gave me a cross look. "Don't be a child, Haze. I've got a girlfriend now. You know orga—"

I put a buttercream frosted fingertip to her lips. "Not another word. Blech. I can't hear about you and Lumpypits without triggering my gag reflex."

"Lupitia," Tizzy said, her speech unhindered by my finger barrier.

I shrugged. "You say potato, I say Loopypoopy." I was still coming to terms with having two familiars under my roof. Ever since that stupid cat's witch managed to get herself jailed after attempting a dangerous ritual to wake up old magic over Halloween, the cat had been staying with us at the new house.

I smiled. I shouldn't. But I did. My bear Shifter fiancé, Ford Baylor and I, had only been able to purchase the house because of an unfortunate murder related to the old magic that nearly killed the entire town of Paradise Falls.

"What's with the heavy sigh?" Tizzy had laid down on her stomach in front of her hot cocoa thimble cup, her little fists balled up under her chin. "You worried Ford has lost that loving feeling?"

"A. I didn't sigh. And B. Mind your own business." Ford had been a little distant the past three weeks, and whenever I asked him if anything was wrong, he'd give me some quick answer about being fine then change the subject.

Argh. I'd spent thirty-seven years of my life without the complication of a relationship, and a few times lately, I had begun to wonder if I shouldn't have waited another thirty-seven.

Kidding. I adored my hunka-hunka-burning-bearman-love. He made my knees knock, my knickers twist, and my knick-knack paddy whack. He certainly knew how to give a witch a bone.

"Yuck, Haze. Just yuck." Tizzy's expression was pure repulsion.

"Cripes." I forgot she could read my thoughts now. Another side effect of having Loopatootie in our lives.

Of course, I am not a traditional witch. I spent almost

as much time in the human world as I ever had in the paranormal. I should have paid more attention in "The Care and Maintenance of Familiars" class in high school.

Tizzy swished her tail back and forth. "I see the tension. So thick I can cut it with my fingernail." She held up a hot pink, neatly manicured claw. "Is that why I'm here eating cake with you instead of Ford?"

I took another bite, this time the lemon tasted as sour as my darkening mood. "No." Maybe. "You're here because you invited yourself along, and Ford had work."

"You're the boss, Haze. It says so on your office door. Chief of Police." She shook her head and puffed her furry cheeks out. "You need to get a hold of your man before he hightails it back to his cave in the deep woods."

"Ford has never lived in a cave," was my lame defense.

"I'm just saying. You have to com-mune-eh-cate," she enunciated. "That's the only way to make a relation-ship work."

"And what, suddenly, makes you a relationship expert?"

"Lupitia and I are coming up on four blissful months."

"More like three and some change. You know that cat is going to break your heart. They are jerks, each and every one of them."

Tizzy gasped and clutched her chest. "I never thought I'd say this, Haze, but you're a racist."

"Am not!" I crossed my arms. "Maybe a specieist, if that's even a thing, but I believe every person is created equal. Lulupussygalore is not a person."

Tizzy's mouth drooped into a frown, and her eyes narrowed. "So...what does that make me then?"

Uh oh. "I'm so sorry, Tiz. I didn't mean..."

"I understand now. To you, I'm a freaking pet, right? I'm property. An item you use to enhance your magic, and nothing more. You think you are the more important of the two of us in this friendship...scratch that... partnership, because we ain't friends anymore, Hazel Kinsey."

"Come on, now. Don't be like that. I didn't mean it the way it sounded." This was going to take more than a day spa pass and a gift certificate for Moo La Latte coffee shop to fix. I might actually have to be nice to... "Lupitia is so nice to you, but she's so mean to me," I whined.

"You said her name right." Tizzy sat back on her hind

legs. "That's a start. You may not like her, Haze, but I love her."

"And I love Ford. That doesn't stop you from making fun of him, calling him names like Fozzy, Teddy, and Winnie all the time." I didn't have any real moral high ground, but I felt like the metaphorical "upper hand" ball had landed in my court. "If you stop talking crap about my boyfriend, I'll stop talking crap about your…cat."

Her chest froze for a few seconds as she held her breath, paused in thought. She tapped her cheek and shook her head. "I can't. I just can't do it. Baloo gives me too much ammunition to pass up."

"Ha ha. Very funny."

She giggled, making a noise that sounded like chittering. "It really is. I have a million of them."

My phone rang. I yanked it out of my purse, eager to end the awful banter between us. "Chief Kinsey," I answered.

"Haze," a deep voice that made my heart race and witchy bits shiver said. It was Ford. I pulled the phone away from my ear. The number wasn't familiar. Whose phone was he calling on?

"Ford," I said when I put the phone back to my ear. "What's wrong with your phone?"

I heard him sigh heavily before he said, "It fell in the water."

"What water?" Had he gone out to the lake? It was near our new place, but it still seemed weird. Maybe he'd been out on a call out there. "Did you have to go in after a rogue beaver shifter?"

"It's a long story."

"I've got time." I drew a heart in the cake crumbs on my plate. Next, I drew a slash through it. Tizzy's eyes widened. I shook my head at her. "Was it work? Is there something I should know about? A dead body?"

"No. No body."

"Cool. Then what's up?"

"I need to talk to you later today."

"Okay." Someone telling you they needed to "talk" was never a good sign. Damn it! Why couldn't he have found a body.

Tizzy jumped up, her eyes widening. "Uh oh," she said.

"What?" I mouthed.

"Got to go, Haze. See ya at home." And she poofed out. Dang it! It was another power she'd gained as a result of living with that crabby cat.

"Haze? You still there?"

"I'm here," I told Ford. "You sound like you have bad news. Do you have bad news? If so, just say it. Rip it off like a bloody bandage."

"Not over the phone."

Son of a witch, it was bad news. The door opened to the bakery and inside walked a processional of felines. I hissed into the phone, "Two tabbies, a Burmese, a British short hair, a Siamese, and two Bombay cats walked into the bakery."

"Is this the beginning of a joke?" He sounded annoyed.

"No." They mixed bag of pussy cats surrounded my table, each one of them casting a judgmental glare at me. "I'm going to have to call you later."

"But Haze—"

"I'm sorry, Ford. I'll make it up to you. Remember the red crotchless panties?" I hung up on him before he could answer.

"Disgusting," the Siamese cat said, its voice decidedly male. It had the classic creamy tan and black markings of its breed. "Hazel Kinsey, you are hereby summoned."

"For what? And who the hell are you to summon me?" Cats were so freaking bossy. Another reason I didn't like Loogiebutt.

"We are the High Familiar Clowder," the British short hair answered.

"Isn't that soup?"

"Not chowder," said the black Bombay on the right of me. "You really are a stupid witch."

"Hey!" I pointed at the smug black cat. "Sticks and stones will break your bones when I pick them up and beat you with them."

He took a step back. "You and your familiar are hereby charged with illegally acquiring an unregistered familiar. Do you deny these charges?"

"I most certainly do." I had no idea what these kitties were going on about. "Who are you again?"

"The High Familiar Clow—"

"Right, right. Clam chowder." I stood up. The seven of them moved in like a well-oiled military unit, surrounding my fuzzy winter boots. "Back off, *gatos*. I'm the chief in this town, and I'll haul you in for Invasion of Personal Space."

"That's not a thing," one of the tabbies said.

"Hey, buddy." I put an indignant hand on my hip. "I make the laws around here." I was beginning to think Tizzy had seen this coming and that's why she'd skedaddled. I was going to kill her when I got home.

"You only enforce the laws. You can't make them." The voice behind the words was shrill and high pitched.

I groaned. Tanya Freaking Geller. The town medical examiner, a healer witch, and a general pain in my bootie. Oh, and she was dating my dad. Bile rose in my throat when I saw her standing in the doorway on the arm of the aforesaid mentioned father.

"Dad." I nodded to my old man, who really, looked anything but old. Again, perks of being a witch. Or a warlock, in his case. He looked young enough to be my brother. Which meant, that even though Tanya was my age, they really did make a nice-looking couple. But why Tanya. She was my nemesis.

I looked at Tanya again. "I don't need any help from you."

"Balderdash," my father said.

"Balderdash to you too," I told him.

The Burmese said, "I'm Balderdash, you ignorant witch."

"At least my name isn't dumb."

My father spoke, intervening before I could step in it again. "What is the HFC doing in Paradise Falls?"

"Yeah." I gave a quick nod. "What are you all doing here?"

"We've come to retrieve and rehabilitate Tisiphone and Lupitia." The black cat on the right of me rubbed his body against my boot. "You will be assigned a new familiar until further notice."

CHAPTER 2

"You have got to be kidding me." I stared at the big eared, hairless, pink-skinned cat sitting on the wooden altar and almost crapped myself. My father had moved our party to the Shifter-Witch Coalition building. The seven cats that made up the familiar high mucky mucks sat in the chairs usually reserved for the coalition.

The naked monstrosity on the altar gave me a bored look.

I pointed at it. "What am I supposed to do with this little mutant?"

"Lonnie is your new familiar," Balderdash said.

I'd been introduced to the entire clowder now, and they all bore ridiculous names. The two Bombay black cats were Deva and Devi. The gray British short hair was Queenie, and the Siamese was named Pluto. The tabbies were John and Jane, which just sounded like aliases to me. Behind them were four witches, two blondes and two redheads along with three warlocks, one with brown hair, one with black, and one was a sandy blonde. They were lined up girl-boy-girl style, and they all stared in my direction, but almost as if they were looking through me not at me. They affected an air of superiority, status quo for their kind, but what really caught my attention was the pulse of power emanating from them as a group.

My creep-o-meter pinged in the red, but I had bigger problems at the moment than the Stepford witches and warlocks.

"I don't need a new familiar. I have a perfectly good squirrel. And why are only cat familiars represented here?" I couldn't believe Tizzy called me a bigot. It seemed like familiars had their own hierarchy based on form.

"Tisiphone is under investigation. Her association with you has been less than an ideal partnership. According to regulation five-oh-one six B, a familiar shall at all times promote a healthy use of sound magic for his or her witch."

"And what makes you think she doesn't?"

"We have had several complaints filed," Devi said. "Like almost burning a hole through the earth's core with hot coffee. Or using magic during a magic ban at Halloween."

"Someone had been murdered," I said in my defense.

Devi's green eyes glowed with condemnation. "We take these complaints seriously."

I cast an accusing glare at Tanya. The redheaded witch shook her head and threw up her hands. "It wasn't me."

"Uh huh."

"It doesn't matter who informed us of the matter, Ms. Kinsey. The point is, we believe that Tisiphone has crossed the line between witch and familiar and familiar. She has developed a bond with the unregistered Lupitia that borders on unprecedented and immoral."

"Homophobes!" I cried out. "Tizzy is allowed to be with who she wants. Love is love, you baboonish bags of wind."

The female tabby Jane stood up on all four paws. "You misunderstand us, Ms. Kinsey. We could care less if Tisiphone has relations with Lupitia. The line she crossed is mystical, not physical. Lupitia has bonded with her."

I must have looked as dumbfounded as I felt, because John said, "Lupitia has become Tisiphone's familiar. She is developing powers she shouldn't have as a result."

"No effing way." I shook my head. "I thought a familiar couldn't be bonded to two witches or a witch and a squirrel in this case. How is that even possible?" Romy Quinn, Lupitia's witch, had been part of a coven that had accidentally almost unleashed hell on Paradise Falls. She, along with her cohort Jenny Weaver, the only two of the coven to survive, had been locked away by my grandmother, the Grand Inquisitor Clementine Battles, in the maximum security magical prison for rogue witches. Lupitia shouldn't have been able to magically bond with a turnip. "Romy Quinn is her witch. Not Tiz."

"Romy Quinn is dead." Deva, the male black cat, leaned forward, his laser sight boring a hole through my skull. Not literally, of course, but I rubbed my forehead anyhow.

I restrained my rising temper and asked, "How did she die?"

"The conditions of her death are not part of the scope of our investigation." Devi, the female Bombay replied. "But we are not here because of Romy Quinn. That is for the Grand Inquisitor's people to investigate. Our only concern is the illegal familiar behavior that has come to pass here in Paradise Falls."

"Look, it's not like we subscribe to *Incarcerated Witch Daily News*. How in the name of the Goddess could Tiz know that Lou-Diamond-Furface was no longer bound to her witch?"

"Who?" Queenie asked.

My father answered, "She means Lupitia."

The hairless wonder, who'd been quiet up until that point, said, "I am your familiar now, Witch Hazel."

"Shut up, Lonnie." I gave the pink beast a warning glare. "Tizzy is my familiar. Period. End of it. You don't get to decide for me."

"Actually..." The flat-faced British shorthair, Queenie, produced a piece of paper. She wiggled her whiskers, and the document appeared in my hand. She had an uppity British voice, like Maggie Smith on Downton Abby or Harry Potter, or really any movie or show Maggie Smith plays in. "If you'll see subsection four-A-E, article thirty-one, the sixth clause, you will note that it is completely at the discretion of the HFC where a familiar is assigned, and completely at our pleasure if we decide to reassign said familiar. In other words, right now there is a chance we may rehabilitate Tisiphone and give her a new witch, but if you continue to fight us, we might not reassign her at all."

Queenie's puckering face reminded me of a butthole. One I wanted to shoot. Which made me wish I carried a gun off duty. I balled my hands into fists. "Which means what exactly?"

My father stepped forward, his tone soft and low. "She will be absorbed into the between."

My temperature went from a comfortable ninety-eight point six to three thousand degrees in two seconds flat. Or at least it felt like it. Granted my clothes hadn't burned off my body, but my anger felt scorching, and if I could have, I would have shot laser beams from my eyes at every single cat, witch, and warlock in the room. I would have missed my dad eventually, but not today.

"This is ridiculous. Tizzy deserves a chance to defend herself. Isn't there some rule in your enormous, ridiculous rule book about that? She didn't try to acquire Luhairy-pits as her familiar to use, she just fell in love. How could she know the damn cat's witch would die? There has to be a concession somewhere for that.

The tabby Jane jumped down to the floor and made her way to the altar, she nested on top of the gazillion-year-old spell book that rested in the center.

She gazed from Lonnie the hairless wonder to me. "You will turn Tisiphone and Lupitia over to the HFC immediately, and you will accept Lonnie as your new familiar."

"Or what?"

She licked her paw and dragged it over her ear and down her face. She actually did it several times in an effort that made her look extremely bored by my panic and pain.

This kind of behavior was exactly the reason I hated cats. Soooooo superior and let's not forget smug.

Queenie, her blandest most condescending great dame tone, answered, "Or you will be stripped of a familiar altogether. You know what they call a witch without a familiar?"

"A muggle," I said.

My father gasped. Tanya Geller blanched. Pluto, the Siamese male, laughed.

There was hope for Pluto.

"They are called humans, you silly, self-destructive witch. Enjoy your mortality."

I tried to hold my composure, but the rise of power in the room as the witches and warlocks began to chant brought me to my knees.

"Stop!" my father shouted. Peripherally, I saw him drop to his knees as their power took him down as well.

"What are...you...doing...to me?" My chest hurt as the pressure of their magic thickened the air.

"Stand up," Lonnie said. His pinched and whiny voice made my teeth hurt.

"I can't," I said through gritted teeth.

"If you reach out to me with your power, I can help you." He held out his paw. His nails were sharp, but he had no style. Not like Tizzy.

"No," I grated out through clenched teeth. "Never."

"Fine," Balderdash said. He meowed really loudly. It sounded more like a cry for help than a rallying cry, but the choking magic dissipated instantly.

I gasped, hungry for air. "I'll never take another familiar."

"We'll see," Balderdash said. "After a few days without magic, you may be singing another tune."

"You can't do that," my dad said. "That's not in your purview. The Grand Inquisitor--"

Balderdash cut him off with a high-pitched mew. "Oh, we know all about your ties to the Grand Inquisitor, but not even your close familial bonds with her can stop us from fulfilling our duty. Subsection four hundred and thirty-seven, article D, clause A, second addendum, the HFC may limit or neutralize a witch's power for seventy hours in order to investigate a complaint."

"At least when I hold someone in jail I read them their rights first." I got to my feet, stumbling as a wave of emptiness washed through me. Had they really stripped me of my powers? Was it even possible? I spent so many years trying not to use magic, but the last several months I'd started to embrace that part of myself that I'd denied for so long. Using minor spells for simple tasks had become like second nature. Besides, I hated cleaning house. Well, anything domestic. Magic had become my bitch.

I stared at the seven HFC members and Lonnie, matching their glare with my own.

"You won't get away with this," I told them.

Queenie jumped down from her chair. "Yes, we will. You tell Tisiphone when you see her that her fate will be worse than she ever imagined if she doesn't turn herself in. She has about as much time as you do. You have three days, Hazel Kinsey. Tisiphone will either turn herself in, or you will lose your powers forever." The word "forever" echoed through the room as the rest of the cats followed Queenie out of the chamber.

Once they'd left, I stomped over to the nearest coalition chair and slumped into the seat. "That was very…"

"Dramatic," Tanya supplied.

"Scary," my dad added.

"Messed up," I said. "But yeah, all the of above."

"Are you really human now?" Tanya asked.

"I don't know. I think so." Goosebumps raised on the surface of my arms as the cooler temperature in the room chilled me.

"Warmth in the air,

Come to me.

Heat and comfort,

So mote it be."

My father waited, his eyes wide and expectant.

I shook my head. "Nothing. I'm still cold."

He sauntered over to me, worry plain on his face. He put his arm around my shoulder. "I'm sorry this is happening to you, sweetheart."

"Dad." I choked on a sob caught in my throat. "I can't...I need Tiz."

"I know," he said. He stroked my hair. "I know."

"What about your mom? She can help, right?" I gazed up at him, but hope died inside me.

Dad shook his head. "She won't get involved. The familiars coexist with the witch community symbiotically. She won't risk the Clowders' ire. Not even for you.

"What's the use of having a grandmother who is large and in charge, if she can't pull some strings for her family."

My dad raised a brow. "She arrested me, her son, and put me in jail for seventeen years."

I grimaced. "Good point. We can fix this, right, Dad?"

His expression was bleak. "We can try."

He put his arm around me, and I sagged against him. "I want to go home."

Tanya smoothed her long, red bouncy hair then fluffed

up the ends. She put her hand on my dad's forearm. "I'll see you later, Kent," she said to him.

I shuddered. I still couldn't get used to her dating my dad. After all, I'd spent my entire childhood hating her and her crowd, and the hate hadn't stopped with time or distance. And now, my nemesis was my dad's new cuddle bunny. It was just all too gross. But again, not my biggest problem.

We'd sort of made an uneasy alliance over Halloween, one that didn't quite break into friendship, but we'd stop being enemies for the most part. The look of pity she gave me now made me wish for the days when she simply hated me.

Dad kissed her cheek when she offered it, then to me, he said, "I'll take you home, Haze." With his arms still around me, he wiggled his fingers, and in a blink, we appeared in my living room.

My home, which used to be the Milan House, had been owned by a founder witch, Agatha Milan. She'd been one of the few members left of the town's founding families until a rogue witch coven killed her.

I still had nightmares about oily tar pits that opened to Hell. Ford still had nightmares about clowns. Halloween had been traumatic for everyone.

Our house was a Victorian masterpiece set on a

picturesque three acres at the south end of the town near Paradise Falls park. I'd fallen in love with it from the moment I'd driven up the driveway to question Agatha. Ford acquired it as an engagement present for me. It had dark walnut, hardwood floors, all original white crown molding separating the rose tint walls with the buff colored ceiling. I didn't change much in the place except the furniture. Agatha Milan's taste was more chic and less comfort. I really liked comfort. Agatha's death was a tragedy, a big loss for Paradise Falls, but I couldn't feel guilty about living in such a beautiful home.

I was happy here. Or at least, I had been.

My dad gave me a quick pat on the shoulder as he let me go. "I have to meet with the coalition and let them know why the High Familiar Clowder is in town. Will you be all right for a while on your own?"

"I lived in the human world for years, Dad. I think I can manage on my own without magic for a bit." I hoped I sounded brave and not like a flipped out, magicless witch. "I'll find Tizzy. We'll make a plan. She'll know what to do." My words sounded hollow even to my own ears.

"Do you know where she might be?"

I blinked and looked at my father. "Who?"

"Tisiphone?"

"Why?" I narrowed my gaze. "Don't even think about turning Tizzy in to save me? She's family, and I would rather live the rest of a short life as a mortal than have her taken away and sent to the between."

"Now, Haze…"

"No," I snapped. "I swear to the goddess, Father, that if you betray Tizzy or me, I will never forgive you."

"You have forgiven me before for worse."

"No, I haven't." I shook my head. Sure, him trying to break the marriage bond with my mother had caused her death, but she'd been a part of a group of witches and shifters practicing druidic rituals of shifter sacrifice. I wasn't terribly sad she was gone. However… "If you give up Tiz to that group of dippy felines, any relationship we might have is over. Promise me. I need you to look me in the eye and tell me you won't help them take her away from me."

My dad stared me straight in the eye, his unlined handsome face grim. "I am your father. If that means I have to do something that you'll hate me for in order to keep you safe then I will." He crossed the floor to me and kissed my forehead.

"I don't need you to keep me safe," I told him. "I need

you to have my back."

"I do, sweetheart." He put his hands together. "I'll be back soon." And he was gone.

I wanted to cry, but the rattling of a key in the front door stopped me from falling apart. All six-foot nine-inches of my man filled the entryway to the living room. Like always, he had to duck under the archway. He wore a pair of sweatpants and a sweatshirt that were two sizes too small for him and looked like they'd been plucked from a lost and found bin. His black hair was messy and damp, and there was an undercurrent of rage behind his light blue eyes.

He stopped when he saw me, almost as if surprised. "Haze." His anger evaporated, replaced by bewilderment and shock. "Your scent. It's...I...don't smell vanilla or rum."

I blinked, aghast at his revelation. Our senior year, my friend Lily and I had gone to a party. We were not in the popular crowd. More freak than geek, but we were determined to have a good time. I got smashed on rum and cream soda, a really gross combination by the way, and kissed the high school quarterback on a dare.

Ford said from the moment our lips touched, he'd picked up my scent. It was a thing that happened to shifters when they found their true mates. For me, the mating scent took on the aroma of a multitude of cinnamon laden desserts. It was like being in a delicious bakery twenty-four-seven when he was around. Only...

"Oh, Goddess," I whispered, unable to stop the tears now. "I can't smell you either."

CHAPTER 3

"**W**HAT'S GOING on, Haze? The mating scent is for life. Nothing but a terrible betrayal could break that bond."

"Why do you assume this is my fault?" Uhm, maybe because I was the one under investigation, sanctions, and oh yeah, my magic had been taken away from me because I refuse to cooperate.

Ford tugged the tight gray sweatshirt over his head, displaying his wide chest, peppered with dark hair, and robbing me of my speech for a second. Well, it was official, the mating scent might be gone, but my parts still wanted his parts.

"What?" Ford asked.

"Why are you wearing clothes that were made for a

toddler?" I recalled our earlier phone conversation. "Did you fall in a lake?"

"Yes," he said. "But I don't want to talk about it right now." He kicked his tennis shoes off. "What happened to our mate bond?"

I am a tough chick, so I did what any tough chick in my situation would do. I cried. Hard.

Ford crossed the room quickly and put his arms around me. I pressed my face against his chest, the sobs coming even harder. "Just tell me what's happening, Haze," Ford said, his voice gentle and comforting. "I can't fix this if you keep me in the dark."

I hiccupped and wiped my wet, snotty face against his hairy pecs. Ford cupped the back of my neck. "Tell me," he said.

"I..." I sniffed. "I d-d-don't know."

"Ewww! Gross," a squeaky voice exclaimed. "I'm in trouble, and you two are making out like a bunch of horny, drunken werebunnies on *Vali's Blot*."

My heart squeezed as my oldest and dearest friend chastised the crap out of me. I stepped away from Ford and wiped my eyes.

"We are not making out," I said.

Ford cast a wary glance in Tiz's direction. "What's *Vali's Blot*?

"It's like Valentine's day, Grizzly Adams," Tiz snapped. "Oh, Haze!" She skittered across the floor, her nails clicking like a speed typist on the hardwood. Her claws bit into my skin as she climbed my pant legs, up the back of my shirt, and onto my shoulder. She tugged at my ear. "Are you crying because of me?"

I shrugged and sniffled. "Maybe."

"Why is Tiz in trouble? What did she do?" A low growl started in his chest and erupted from his throat. "And why has it broken our mating bond?"

"I didn't do anything!" Tizzy squealed. "I won't let them take me, Haze." She grabbed two handfuls of my hair and yanked. "Never!"

"That hurts," I protested.

She let go. "Sorry."

I rubbed the two bumps on my scalp. "I won't let them take you, Tiz. You're my familiar, and even more, you're my family. We'll figure this out."

"Now that you two have hashed that out, can someone please tell me what the nine levels of hell you guys are talking about and what it has to do with us?"

"I don't know why the scent thing isn't working." Once again, I was desperately close to tears.

"Wait a minute," Tiz said. "You guys have lost your bond?" She brushed back my hair and looked inside my ear.

I flicked her finger away. "Stop that."

"I need to examine you, Haze." She yanked my lobe firmly. "Hold still. I thought the HFC cut me off from you, but it's worse than that, isn't it?"

Getting probed by a flying squirrel ranked right up there on the "last-thing-I-wanted list," but since the very last things on that list would be to lose Ford or Tizzy, I gave her the nod. "Fine. Do what you gotta."

I regretted my words the instant she stuck a finger in my ear. Ack! Next, she scurried over my head feeling all the bumps and dents in my scalp. She crawled around to my chest, balancing one foot on each boob. Thank heavens for padded bras, because otherwise, I'd have four little holes on each of the girls. She pried my mouth open and stuck her head in far enough her ears tickled the roof.

"Gah," I protested.

"Hold still," she chided. She pulled my peepers apart next and stared into each one. At the end of her examination, she darted her tongue out and licked my eyeball.

I yelped and stumbled back. I would have knocked Tiz off me at that point, but she'd already launched herself onto the couch.

"What did you do, Hazel Kinsey?" Her tone bordered on accusing.

I rubbed my eyelid. "I let a rodent lick my eyeball."

"Your magic." She pointed her finger at me. "It's gone."

Ford's brow furrowed with worry as he put his hands on my shoulders. "What is she talking about, Haze? How can your magic disappear?"

"It's Tizzy's fault. If she hadn't fallen for that crabby ball of fluff, none of this would have happened."

"But I luuuuurve her," Tizzy proclaimed.

"I'm all for love," I told her, but you shouldn't have let her bond with you. Familiars bond with witches. They don't bond with other familiars." I hated that I sounded like a public service announcement for the damn HFC. "You know your own magic has been changing beyond that of a familiar. There are rules, and you broke them. And now, the League of Annoying

Cats have stripped me of my witch powers until I rat you out or you turn yourself in."

"They did what?" Ford gripped my upper arms, not hard, but firm. "What do you mean they've stripped you of your powers?"

"Just what it sounds like." I sighed. "For the next seventy-two hours, and maybe for eternity, I am a human. A freaking mortal." I shook my head. "Oh Goddess, help me."

"I won't let that happen," Tiz said. "I'll turn myself in right now."

I grabbed her by the bushy tail before she could even think about blinking out on me. "You will do no such thing, Tisiphone. I cannot go through eternity with a hairless, shriveled monster named Lonnie as my sidekick."

"Lonnie!" Tizzy spat, the gross loogie landed on my hand. "That cat is a total jackhole!"

"Ah!" I let her tail go, shaking the clinging spit to the floor. "That's so disgusting."

"Not as disgusting as Lonnie. He's a Grade A douchebag. You know, the kind your grandma used to use, red swollen bladder, long unhygienic tubing, and a nozzle that smells perpetually of vinegar and—"

"Stop. I get the picture." An image of Clementine Battles seasoning her salad in the shower flashed into my mind. Ack. " Vividly," I said. "So vivid I might need therapy." I shook my head and sat down on the couch next to Tizzy. "What are we going to do? I can't let you turn yourself in. Even if it means I lose my magic."

Another growl diverted my attention from the squirrel. I looked up at Ford. His eyes were narrowed on me, and there was an angry snarl on his lips. "And what about us?"

"What do you mean? We'll be fine." Toads and newt eyes, losing my powers was going to lose me Ford. What if the only reason he was with me was because of the mating scent? It could make a shifter pretty darn obsessive. What if he decided he wanted to be with someone else? Or Goddess forbid, what if he caught the mating scent with someone else? I couldn't compete with another shifter if he caught her scent. "I'll get my magic back," I promised. "I'll figure this all out so we can be together." I looked from Ford to Tizzy. "All of us."

Ford smoothed his hair back from his eyes. "Hazel."

A chiming tune of *Do You Believe In Magic* began to play through the house. It was the doorbell. I pivoted to Tiz. "You've got to go."

She nodded and disappeared.

"I'm going to get dressed," Ford said. "But we're not done talking about this."

"Of course, we're not," I agreed.

He brushed his lips lightly against my forehead and walked down the hall toward the foyer. I heard his heavy footfalls against the stairs as he ascended to the second floor.

I was on my own with whomever was at the door. The chimes began again. "I'm coming!"

My stomach knotted as I looked through the peephole. I saw nothing and no one. I stepped back. Weird. The doorbell sounded again. Hellfire and brimstone, was I being haunted? Again?

When the doorbell started once more, I flung the door open. "Who's out here?"

"It took you long enough, Ms. Kinsey," a low, low booming voice from the area of my feet said.

I looked down. Sitting on my stoop was a fluffy snow-ball-looking cat the size of a grapefruit. "What are you supposed to be? The king of the itty bitty kitty committee? And do you pay James Earl Jones for your voice over work, because, damn, son, you got a deep voice."

"You insolent witch. I'll have you know, I'm Leonidus the Enforcer, a teacup Persian, and a hired gun for the High Familiar Clowder."

My Goddess, he was feisty for something no bigger than Ford's palm. I resisted the urge to pick him up. His adorableness was that overwhelming. "You are delightfully cute. Has anyone ever told you that?"

"I am not cute, you overgrown witch. You will treat me with respect?"

"Or what?" I guffawed. "You'll take away my magic? Oh, wait. That already happened. Hit the road, Frosty."

"Ha ha," the cat said. "We need to talk."

"Uh, do you have a mouse in your pocket? Because there is no we." I closed the door. When I turned away, a booming thunder shook the walls. Chunks of wood hit my back and knocked me down. I face-planted the floor. "What the fu—"

A white cloud of evil cuteness put his tiny paw over my mouth. "You have no choice in this. You will talk to me."

"Look here, mini-Darth, you're going to pay for that door." I tried to get up, but it was as if someone stuck me to the ground with Super Glue. My limbs refused to move. I fought against panic. "Get your toes off me, Stay-Puff."

Four claws poked into my upper lip. "I don't think you understand the damage I can do to you." He retracted his claws. "But you'll learn."

I forced a smile, trying to ignore the blood droplets peppering my upper lip. "You're even more endearing when you go all tyrant. Just like a miniature Napoleon."

"Napoleon wasn't that short," Leonidus quipped. "He just surrounded himself with tall people."

"Sure." I would have nodded if my neck wasn't paralyzed as well. "Whatever you say."

"You can keep being a smart-aleck, or you can talk to me."

"This is how I talk."

A roar from the staircase stirred the wind in the foyer to blow the teacup Persian's hair around. He turned his gaze to where the roar had originated then back to me, his jade green eyes wide.

"There's a giant bear on the steps, isn't there?" I couldn't look, obviously. Not with my body paralyzed, but I knew the sound of Ford fully-shifted into were-bear form.

"Will he try to eat me?"

I blinked because it was the only expression I could pull off. Stupid cat had paralyzed every part of me but my mouth and eyes. "And risk getting a furball caught in his throat? Yes, I think he will." I blinked again. "Let me up, and I'll put in a good word for you."

I could feel the heat from Ford's large body as he rumbled his way toward us.

"Fine," Leonidus said. "Let her go!" he shouted out the door. Feeling came back to my body. I rose up on my elbows and crane my neck to watch the huge bear taking menacing steps in our direction.

Leonidus gave me a sharp glare. "This isn't over."

I sat up, stretched my shoulders, and gave the hairy Mussolini my best, I don't give a flying fig look. "Fix the door on your way out." I waved with just my fingers. "Buh-bye."

The minute the mini-mop skated out the empty space where my door used to be, all the wood that had broken apart reformed into a solid piece of Victorian craftsmanship.

I heard bone crunching and sucked in my breath. Ugh. I hated the sounds Ford's body made as it remade itself from man to animal and back to man, but...

Hubba, hubba. Ford sat on stairs now, completely naked, and I mean completely. Hot diggity. I wiped the corner of my mouth to make sure I wasn't drooling.

Ford shook his head. "Who was that tiny tyrant?"

"Leonidus the Enforcer, apparently." I walked over to him and straddled his thighs.

He met my gaze, stroking my hair from my shoulder. "You're kidding."

I slid my hand down his chest. "Would I do that?"

"You would." He ran his fingers through my hair. "You have some blood above your lip." He licked the claw marks, tasting me. "I'm going to kill that little bastard." His eyes softened at the corners. "I don't know what I'd do if anything happened to you." He cupped the back of my head and tugged, bending my neck back, to run his lips over my skin.

I moaned, my va-jay-jay screaming yay-yay, as I ground my groin against his. Since he was naked, his arousal writhed between us. The look of pure lust in his eyes choked at my emotions. He still wanted me. But how long could it last without our mating scent? I wanted to believe that we didn't need it to be together, but I think a part of me always felt that magic was the only reason he would mate with someone like me.

As if he could see the wheels turning in my head and wanted to send them to a grinding halt, Ford yanked my shirt over my head, his lips finding their way beneath my collar bone. I moved against him, thrilled when he moaned with pleasure at my efforts.

"Oh. My. Goddess!" Tizzy shrieked, rudely interrupting our sexy time. "I am in crisis here, and you two are boning like porn stars."

I grabbed my shirt to cover Ford's erection. It looked like a camping tent for beavers. "We weren't boning," I protested. "Not yet, anyhow." If she'd have given us a few more minutes, we would have totally boned.

"I don't have time for your horny nonsense," Tizzy said. This coming from a squirrel who was ruled by her hormones. "I. Am. Freaking. Out."

"Did something else happen?"

Tizzy's brown eyes grew large and glassy. "Lupitia."

"What about Loser-ita?"

Her lower lip quivered, and she sobbed, "Lupitia is gone, Haze. She's vanished off the face of the earth."

CHAPTER 4

"ARE YOU SURE she didn't run away on her own." Ford had gone upstairs and put on clothes, while Tiz and I sat in the kitchen. I poured myself a cup of coffee, wishing I had a couple of Xanax to go with it.

Tizzy prostrated herself on the center island. "She wouldn't have run away."

"Not even to hide?"

"She was hiding already! I had a tree all set up for us out in the woods near the waterfall. I even packed her favorite foods. I didn't even complain about the stinky salmon."

"Maybe she decided to try her luck on her own."

"I can't feel her, Haze." Tizzy looked tired. Worn down.

"Our bond. It's weakening. I can't feel her and…I can't feel you."

"Those stupid cats," I muttered. "This is exactly the reason your better off without—"

"Don't say it," Tizzy cried. "I'm not better off without her. Or you."

"Did you know you were breaking the rules when you asked me to let Loopty-loo live with us?"

"No." My familiar averted her gaze and nodded her head. "Yes."

"Damn it, Tiz." I smacked the counter. "We've got no leg to stand on if the chowder is in the right."

"Clowder." She gave me a sour look. "I didn't think they'd find out, but when Romy, Lupitia's witch, died in prison I started gaining witch magic…" She shrugged.

"What do you mean by witch magic?"

"You know." She wiggled her pretty pink nails at me, poofed out of sight, then poofed back, only she was on the other side of the center island now. "Witch magic."

Goddess help us. "I knew you were getting stronger with your powers, but you didn't tell me they were beyond your normal familiar stuff. I just thought you were super juiced."

"So let me get this straight," Ford said as he entered the room. "The squirrel broke the rules, you lost your magic, and now are mate scent is gone. Does that about cover it?"

He wore jeans, an emerald green T-shirt, and boots. In other words, clothing that actually fit. I still wanted to know why he'd arrived home in such disarray, but that could wait until we figured out my familiar problem.

"So glad Fuzzy Wuzzy is up to speed," Tizzy said. "Now, what are we going to do about it, Haze? What's the big plan?"

"First…I'm going to finish this cup of coffee." I took a sip. "Ow." And burned my lip. And, because I was human for the moment, it really hurt.

"Are you okay?" Ford asked.

"I'm fine." Really, though, all these little pains that I wouldn't normally be bothered with freaked me out.

"The plan?" Tizzy prodded.

"Well, first, we need to get a hold of that rule book. The one sheet they showed me had a gazillion-million clauses, sub-clauses, and whatever, so there has to be a loophole we could exploit somewhere."

She threw up her hands. "That's your big play. You want to go all legal eagle on the HFC?"

I winced. "I'm smart. And I was an FBI agent for a lot of years. I have training in the law."

"In criminal law, not familiar protocols." Tizzy stomped her back feet. It sounded like rain. "We need a better plan."

"It wouldn't hurt to be versed in the rules," Ford said. "You need ammunition."

"I'm not a gun." Tizzy harrumphed.

"Look, as long as we keep you off the HFC's radar, we have seventy-two hours." I looked at the clock. "Well, more like sixty-eight hours to figure this out before the situation becomes dire." Wow, four hours had passed. I wished I had a spell to slow down time.

"What does that mean?" Ford asked.

I eased back and let out a slow breath. With as much nonchalance as I could muster, I said, "If they don't have Tizzy in custody in that time frame, and I don't accept a new familiar, my human status will be permanent. No biggie." I stood up, suddenly jittery and wishing I'd skipped the caffeine.

I braced myself for the wrath of Ford. After all, he'd been a might growly for the past several weeks, and more than once since he'd arrived home today I keenly felt his disapproval. Instead, he walked over to me and pulled me into his arms.

"We'll get through this, babe." He cupped my chin and placed a tender kiss on my lips. "We'll figure this out. Together."

Relief flooded me, and I gripped Ford tightly. "I love you," I told him.

In response, he kissed me again, his hot lips melding against mine. I wanted nothing more than to freeze the moment and stay in his arms, our mouths pressed together in an eternal kiss.

"Great, glad we're wasting time on the," Tizzy finger quoted the next word, "*important* matters. I'm very inspired."

"I'm having a bad day," I told her. "Can you give me a break?" I shook my head. "I'm sorry. I didn't mean that. I know this isn't all about me. This thing affects all of us."

"Damn skippy. Like the fact that my girlfriend is missing, possibly worse. Now, how are we going to find Lupitia? That's priority one."

"I am still the chief of police. I can call in an all-points bulletin." I looked at Ford. "Who's on tonight?"

"Alice Michaels and Rhonda Petry. Rhonda's a pretty good tracker."

Alice, a witch, and her partner Rhonda, a werecougar, worked well together. They didn't let Witch-Shifter politics get in the way of doing solid police work.

I nodded to Ford. "Okay. It's settled then. I'll call the station. Tiz, you figure out some way to get the damn rule book. And Ford…"

"I'll call my father."

"You're dad?"

"You know he's a business lawyer. If anyone could translate legal speak, it's him."

"There." I gave a nod to Tiz. "We have a plan."

BY THREE O'CLOCK IN THE MORNING, WE'D CALLED IT A night. My officers would ring me if they found the cat. We agreed not to talk to Bryant Baylor, Ford's dad until we had the familiar rule book in hand. Well, I whined, complained, and bemoaned until Ford agreed. While his mother Anita loved me, Bryant didn't approve of his son, heir to the *Arcturus*, marrying a witch.

I tried not to think about the fact that the only thing

Bryant would hate more than his son marrying a witch was his son marrying a human.

Ford wrapped his arms around me when we'd settled into the bed. The clock read three-thirty, which meant, I only had sixty hours left to solve my familiar crisis. Twelve hours had passed since I'd lost my magic, since I'd faced the possibility of losing Tiz, and in that time, I'd accomplished diddly-squat. I take that back, diddly-squat would have been a step up from the absolute nothingness I'd accomplished.

"Penny for your thoughts."

"Inflation," I reminded him. I snuggled my face into his chest and tried to comfort myself in his warmth and steady heartbeat.

"A nickel?" he prodded.

"I don't have any idea how to make this right."

He ran his fingers down my back in soothing strokes. "Sleep now. In a few hours, we'll work on making this right. Tonight, you need to rest."

I curled my body in tighter to him and inhaled deeply. Ford smelled of strawberry shampoo and raspberry body wash. I sighed. I already missed the scent of cinnamon and vanilla that normally permeated my senses when he was near. "What will happen if the mating scent doesn't return?"

"We'll cross that bridge when we come to it."

"But, you were supposed to marry Greta." Greta was another bear Shifter in town. She'd dated Ford in high school. Everyone always expected the quarterback and his cheerleader to mate. But I got drunk at a high school party and changed his life with one sloppy kiss. Then I'd moved away from Paradise Falls for seventeen years, never realizing that I'd ruined his life.

"Greta was a long time ago."

"Maybe this could be your chance." The words stuck in my throat. I'd loved Ford since my sophomore year of high school, but he never even knew who I was until fate forced him to pay attention.

The muscles in his arms bunched, squeezing me hard enough to hurt. "My chance for what?"

"Ease up, Ford. Without my magic, I'm as fragile as a human."

He relaxed his hold. "What are you saying, Haze?"

"I'm saying, you didn't have a choice when it came to me. If I hadn't kissed you on a dare, you would have had a whole 'nother life. One that involved bear cubs. One that would have made your dad happy."

"Oh, because the mate scent is the only reason I'm with you, right?" He sounded angry.

I pressed on. "Maybe."

Ford abruptly let me go. He got out of bed, put on his boxers, and grabbed his pillow. "We don't even know if this is permanent, and you're already trying to get rid of me."

"I'm not trying to get rid of you. It's the last thing I want. It's just…"

"You don't believe that I love you. You think it's all chemical." He shook his head then turned his back on me.

"Where are you going?"

"To think," he said. "Isn't that what you wanted?" He slammed the bedroom door on his way out.

"Great," I muttered. What I really wanted was to be back in his arms where it felt safe. I spent the next twenty minutes crying myself to sleep.

CHAPTER 5

A T SEVEN-THIRTY IN the morning, I woke up. Alone. Ford's pillow was back, which meant he'd come in some time while I was sleeping, probably to get his clothes. I had fifty-six hours now to figure out the situation with Tizzy and her gal pal.

Neither Alice or Rhonda had called me, which meant Drops-of-Lupiter was still missing. I had to consider that the HFC might already have her. I mean, Leonidus, for a little guy, was pretty powerful. Maybe he and his witch, because I'm sure he had one lurking nearby when he'd paralyzed me, could have cast a strong location spell. At least, that's what I would have done if I still had my powers.

If the clam chowder had Loopity-doo, how long would it take to use her to get to Tiz? I couldn't let that happen.

Feeling stiff, I stretched. The bones in my shoulders popped. The right one hurt from where I'd slept on it. And my back, where the door hit had blasted me, hadn't hurt too badly when I went to bed, but now it felt like a solid bruise. I sat up, my lower back complaining as I straightened.

Something wasn't right. I'd never woke up with these kinds of pains before.

I dangled my legs over the side of the bed. My knees hurt too. Why did I feel like someone had come in during the night and beat the crap out of me?

My hair fell forward as I pushed myself to a stand. Strands of silver, not much, but enough to get my attention, sparkled in my blonde hair.

My heart pounded against the inside of my chest, and my breath became labored as I stumbled to the master bathroom. I grabbed the vanity counter to steady myself, turned on the light, and gasped at what I saw in the mirror.

It wasn't the tiny scabs starting to form over the claw marks or the red bruise on my cheek. No. It was worse than wounds. Fine lines etched my brow, the corners of my eyes had the start of crow's feet wrinkles, my lips looked a little less plump, and the creases in my neck had deepened. I gasped again as I noted tiny blonde whiskers at the corner of my mouth and one under my chin.

"Nooooooooo!" I yelled. I moved closer to the mirror, which only made the detail blurry. I touched my face. The texture of my skin had lost its youthful smoothness.

The phone rang. I ran to the bedside table as quick as I could and snatched it up. The number, again, was unknown.

"Hello," I answered, my voice shaky with shock.

A booming voice I recognized as Leonidus the Enforcer said, "Have you looked in the mirror yet, Ms. Kinsey?"

"What did you do to me, you miniature monster?" I hissed.

"Me? Nothing. Did you really think you could lose your magic and not age to your actual years? What you're experiencing is what most human women experience when they near their forties." He chuckled. The sound of his delight sent a chill down my back. I can't believe I ever thought he was cute! "Just count your lucky stars you weren't ancient. A dried corpse is hard to come back from."

"When I get my magic back, I'm going to make you pay, gremlin."

"Tick-tock, Kinsey. Time is running out, and if you don't give up Tisiphone, it won't stop running out for you. You'll die a lonely old woman while everyone you love lives on."

"Look, you abominable snow turd—"

He hung up.

I threw my phone on the bed and screamed my frustration.

Do You Believe In Magic chimed through the house.

I went to the window overlooking the front porch. I couldn't see the front door, but a four-door, burgundy sedan was parked out front.

"Dad," I whimpered. I opened up the window and shouted. "I'll be down in a minute. Go on in."

I took off my nightgown and noticed a dark purple bruise on my collar bone, and right below, my girls were sagging a little. Not a lot, mind you, but enough for me to notice. I put on a bra to keep them in their proper place. Man, aging sucked. How did human women live like this?

I tried a pair of jeans on, but they were tight in the thighs and the waist, areas of my body that had thickened up during my sleep. I was seriously regretting yesterday's cake tasting. I opted for black sweatpants and one of Ford's t-shirts. A light blue one that always made his blue eyes sparkle.

Where was Ford? Why hadn't he answered the door? Maybe he'd taken one gander of me in bed, looking like a middle-aged woman, and decided he really was better off with someone else. What a superficial jerk!

Goddess guide me, I needed to get my shit under control.

"Haze," my dad hollered from the bottom of the stairs. "You coming down."

"Be right there!" I brushed my teeth with Ford's toothbrush, because A, my mouth tasted like a beaver pooped in it, and B, as a witch, I'd never needed to worry about things like brushing my teeth, so I didn't even own a toothbrush.

I checked my smile after. My teeth were slightly worn flat and not as white as usual, but otherwise, they looked healthy. Thank the Goddess. I don't know what I'd have done if they'd rotted with my overnight aging.

When I walked downstairs, my knees ached a little with each step. Damn, getting older sucked. My dad waited for me at the bottom. I tried to smile. "Hey, Dad."

"Oh, Hazel," he said when he took in my appearance.

"What happened to your face? Why do you have a shiner? I worried the aging would happen without your magic, but I didn't think about injuries."

"You knew me getting old was a possibility and didn't tell me?"

"I didn't want to add to your stress. We can't concern ourselves with this right now."

"Every time I move it's a concern." The aches weren't horrible, not like the bruises, but they were an annoying reminder of years of stress that police work had put on my joints that no longer magically healed.

"The coalition wants to speak with you."

"Why? So they can yell at me for being an irresponsible witch? I feel bad enough as it is. Unless they can help, I'll take a hard pass for the next…" I pulled my phone from my pocket and looked at the time on the screen, "Fifty-five hours and some change."

"They don't want to yell at you, Haze. They want to help."

"Right," I scoffed. "Bryant Baylor is a bear with a bug up his big, furry behind about me. He would love to have an excuse to get rid of me. Robert Peirce still blames me for the fall of Adele Adams, even though she was an evil witch responsible for several deaths in town, and Tanya and I have never been close."

"Haze," my father warned.

"No," I told him, already on a roll. "Tanya and I barely tolerate each other, and we only do it for you. I don't know Mary Lowe well, but since she is the alpha for the cat Shifters, and never did a damn thing to help Lily when her brother was murdered, I don't think I can expect a lot of sympathy there. And Mike Crandall…well, Mike is a weremole. Unless he is going to dig me out of this situation, I don't see how he can help. The coalition is worthless. Less than worthless," I cried. "You are the only person on the coalition who isn't a complete uppity, incompetent ass-hat."

When I finished, I heard the clearing of a throat at the end of the foyer.

"Oh, hellfire and save the matches." The entire coalition, the one I'd just verbally trashed, stared at me. "Kidding," I said to them. "Human humor." I looked at my father for a rescue, but he shook his head, disappointment marring his handsome features.

Goddess on toast, my father looked years younger than me.

"I'm sorry," I said.

"I'm not the one you need to apologize to," he replied.

I clamped my lips tight then relaxed them. "I'm sorry you all had to hear that," I said as sincerely as I could muster.

"But you're not sorry you said it," Bryant Baylor said, picking up on the nuance of my apology.

I met his angry gaze with a fire of my own. "It's hard to be sorry about the truth."

My dad reached out and squeezed my good shoulder. "Enough, Haze. Right now, we need all the friends we can get."

I didn't see a single friend in the room. Lily had moved to Missouri, which up until yesterday had been a blink away, and Tiz... I looked around. Where was Tiz? Hiding somewhere good, I hoped. Somewhere none of these ass-ninnies could find her.

I pulled my shoulders back and lifted my chin. I might be losing my flexibility, but I would not lose my dignity. "Can I offer you all a drink? Coffee? Tea? Whiskey?" I pushed past the logjam of coalition members to make my way toward the kitchen. It was only eight in the morning now, but whiskey was starting to sound like the most palatable option.

CHAPTER 6

ROBERT PIERCE STARED at me from across the living room. He perched near the foyer, his arms crossed as he leaned back against the wall. Mary Lowe and Mike Crandall sat on either side of the couch. Bryant Baylor stood near the plush, brown chair Ford loved. Maybe he could smell his son on that particular piece of furniture. Tanya sat in the other chair, one that was firmer but complimented Ford's.

In other words, my chair.

I took a drink of coffee, hoping to wash the bitter taste from my mouth.

My dad stood by me as we faced the lot of them.

Finally, Mary Lowe broke the silence. "We would like to help you, Chief Kinsey."

"Why?" I asked.

My question took her aback. "In the past eight months, you have saved this town from two major disasters. Mundane crimes, which in the past have been ignored by the police force, are now being solved. While there are still tensions between the shifters and witches, I've also seen a lot of progress. Your implementation of a partnering a shifter with a witch or warlock out on patrol has helped Paradise Falls realize a steep decrease in severe injuries and fatalities during police calls." She looked me in the eye and gave me a thin-lipped smile. "In other words, while you are abrasive, undiplomatic, and a general pain in the ass, you have been good for our town."

My mouth dropped open. I closed it. It dropped open again. "That was surprisingly honest."

"Yes," Mary said. "It was." The corner of her mouth tugged up in what I could swear was a genuine smile.

I nodded to her. "I can work with that. Do the rest of you feel the same?"

There were general mutterings of agreement, except for Bryant and Robert. I stuck my tongue out at Robert, and his face reddened.

"Okay," I said. "I'm ready to listen."

"Good," my dad said. "Tanya brought her copy of the familiar rules."

I nodded. "Ford says that Bryant might be able to sort through all the double speak and find a way to circumvent the HFCs ruling."

Bryant gave me a strange look, but said, "I'll see what I can do."

"Excellent." My dad turned to Mary Lowe. "You get your best trackers out in the woods where Lupitia was last seen. There's too much territory for Haze's police force to cover."

Mary stood up. "I'll start the phone tree and have my people gather at the edges of the park. We will work our way in. Do you have something of hers that we can scent?"

"There's a cat bed in Tiz's room, will that work?"

She nodded. "Yes. That will do."

My dad addressed Mike Crandell next. "I need you to recruit some of your more trusted people to spy on the High Familiar Clowder."

Mike nodded. "I have a few that I can rely upon."

Bryant and Mary both raised their brow, giving Crandall appraising looks.

The weremole smiled. "We're small, but we're effective."

"And now for Pierce," my dad said. He sounded annoyed. It was nice to know I wasn't the only one Pierce affected that way. "Robert, I'd like you to develop a rapport with the clowder's witches. Maybe feel them out to see if any of the HFC members can be swayed."

"I've already told you that I want no part of this plan of yours, Kent. Unlike the other members of the coalition, I don't think Chief Kinsey has been an asset to our town. On the contrary, I think she's a menace."

Bryant Baylor stood up. "You are a member of the coalition, which means, you are bound by any vote. Majority rules. You were outvoted."

"We already had this discussion, Robert," my father said. "We agreed—"

"You agreed," Pierce countered. "It's easy to go up against the High Familiar Clowder when you have nothing to lose. Tanya and I both have familiars. We risk the HFC taking them away if we interfere. They don't like to be defied."

"I may not have a familiar." My dad walked over and stood next to me. He put his arm around my shoulder. "But I have plenty to lose if things don't work out."

Awww! "Thanks, Dad."

"You got it, pumpkin." He looked around at the group. "We have fifty-three hours and twenty-eight minutes before Hazel's seventy-two hours are up. Check in if you find something. If not, meet here tomorrow morning at seven—"

"Eight," I interjected.

"Eight," Dad agreed. "I'll bring bagels."

"And donuts." I smiled.

Dad kissed my cheek. "And donuts."

Tanya gave me a once over. "You might want to skip the donuts until you get your powers back."

I glared at her. "I was just starting to not hate you."

She grinned. "I don't hate you either." She grabbed my dad's arm. "Let's go, Kent. Bryant," she told the bear alpha. "Let's meet at the coalition building at noon. I'll bring my book."

After quick, perfunctory goodbyes, the six of them departed, and I was finally alone with my aging body along with its little idiosyncrasies.

"Awesome." I moved my pity party into the kitchen.

Tizzy materialized onto the center island. "Are

they gone?"

"Where have you been? I was worried."

She glared at me, then shrieked. "What has happened to you? You're hideous."

"Don't be mean."

"I'm just teasing. For a human, you're aging remarkably well. Other than the bruise, of course."

"You might have to get used to me with graying hair and wrinkles."

"Goddess forbid, Haze. That's what hair dye and Botox is for."

"Har har." I reached out and stroked her tail. Tizzy looked like she'd gained a couple of years in age too. Her fur was less shiny, her nail polish was chipped, and there was a dullness in her eyes I'd never seen before. "We're really in a mess, aren't we? Any news on Ludicrous."

Tizzy frowned. "Nothing. I can still feel the power between us, even if I can't feel where she is, which means if the HFC has her, they haven't severed our bond yet."

"About that. You knew she'd joined her power to yours, didn't you?"

Tizzy bobbed her head. "About a month after she'd moved in. We were playing cuddle sticks one night, and wham, it was like our souls joined together. I'd never felt anything like it. At first, I just thought it was our love, but the first time I performed magic I shouldn't have been able to do…"

"Like apparating."

"For example," she said. "I knew something else was going on. Lupitia was freaked out when her tie to Romy completely vanished. She called the prison then and found out Romy had killed herself."

"Her death was a suicide?"

"Yes." Tizzy clasped her hands together. "Lupitia cried for days. I guess Romy couldn't take being in prison. It was too much to be without magic and Lupitia."

"Wow." It made me feel a little guilty for being so crappy to the cat. "Why didn't you tell me, Tiz?"

"I didn't want her sent away to be reassigned. She's my Helen of Troy, and like Paris, I would fight a war to be with her."

"That's very romantic, Tiz, but you still should have told me."

"I know." She crawled up my arm and buried her head under my hair. "Speaking of romance, what happened between you and the Care Bear last night. He left this morning looking more frowny than usual."

"It's complicated."

"I do complicated. Spill."

"I told him that if our mate scent doesn't come back, he might be off the hook with me." I felt a sharp tug on my hair. "Ouch."

"You really do need a keeper, Haze. That bear may be a constipated pain in my tail, but he would die for you."

"Yeah, when it was magic holding us together. Without it, what do we have?"

"Look at us. Two peas in a pod. Blowing up our life, one bad decision after another."

"At least, we're together."

She rubbed her nose against my neck. "I'm scared, Haze."

"Me too."

"You're always such a comfort," she said dryly, then swished her tail in my face.

"I miss Lily." I stroked Tizzy's tail as it curled around my throat. "Do you miss Lily?"

"I miss Lily so much," my familiar said, "but I don't miss that monster she calls a dog."

"Smooshie is sweet."

She poked me with a claw. "Smooshie tried to eat me."

"She was just playing with you, Tiz."

"That vicious beast played me right up the nearest tree." Tizzy crawled down into my lap and curled into a little ball.

"I'd love to hold you all day, girl, but I'm not getting any younger."

"That statement has never been truer."

Do You Believe In Magic chimed again.

"I used to love that doorbell," I said.

"I'm out of here." Tizzy disappeared.

I sighed. Heavily. I wished I could disappear as well. "I miss magic."

"Open the door, witch!" Leonidus yelled. Damn, he had some lungs for a munchkin. "I know you're in there."

I walked to the door slowly, because—jerk. I would not be bossed around by a wad of cotton with a mouth.

When I finally opened the door, the minuscule kitty looked ready to demolish tiny cities with his rage. "Can I help you, cutie-pants?"

His body vibrated like a massage pillow. "Quit calling me cute!"

Bored with the banter, I asked him, "What do you want?"

"The High Familiar Clowder has sent me to fetch you."

"Tell them they can pull the stick out of your butt and fetch that."

"Do not push me, witch. You know what I'm capable of." He narrowed his eyes at me, Goddess, making him even more precious. At that moment, I realized the appeal of cat videos in social media.

I smiled.

"Do not smile at me!"

"That's going to be a tough one," I admitted. Power choked me and drove me to my knees. "Hey, that hurts, cotton swab. These new human joints suck, so quit slamming me to the ground."

"Enough, Leo," a woman with a platinum blonde, A-cut bob said. "We're supposed to escort Ms. Kinsey to the clowder, not damage her."

"She won't stop calling me cutesy names, Pearl. You know I hate that."

"You are cute. After two hundred years, you think you'd be used to people fawning over you."

"It doesn't mean I have to like it," he said to his witch.

On a good day I might find their banter adorable, but this wasn't a good day. "Uhm. I hate to interrupt your conversation, but can I get up now. Seriously, these knees ain't what they used to be."

"Sorry," the woman said. From head to toe, she was dressed in black, a stark contrast to her almost silvery hair. "I'm Pearl Vickers. You've met, Leo. He's my familiar."

"Lucky you," I muttered as I struggled to my feet. "Why does Team Familiar want to see me?"

"We aren't told why they want anything." Pearl's tone sounded a little disgruntled. "Our job is to enforce their wishes, not have an opinion about them."

"I see." Questioning them would get me nowhere, better to just see what the kitten brigade wanted. Besides, I might learn something useful. I sighed with resignation. "Let me get my shoes on and grab my purse."

CHAPTER 7

I'D LEFT A NOTE for Ford and Tizzy, though I only addressed it to Ford. I couldn't afford to have the HFC think I was in contact with my squirrely-girl. Pearl and Leonidus took me in a black sports car that, if it hadn't been inanimate, I might have thought it was one of Pearl's family members. Sleek, sexy, and just a hint of dangerous.

I put my head against the window when we pulled onto Elysium street and perked up when Pearl parked at Lolo's Diner. "Isn't this place a little crowded for a meeting? Not that I'm complaining. I could go for some dessert and some coffee."

"The bosses have rented the place out for the day. Apparently, your Shifter-Witch Coalition told them to get a place of their own."

"Pearl," Leo said disapprovingly.

"What?" She shrugged. "It's not anything Ms. Kinsey can't find out on her own. I mean, I'm certain someone will tell her that Kent Kinsey told Balderdash to go find his own litter box to piss in." A hint of a smile played at the corners of her mouth.

"Loose lips," the snowball said.

Pearl rolled her eyes. "Let's get you inside," she told me. "I'm sure whatever they have planned for your afternoon will be thrilling and educational."

I walked into Lolo's. Pearl and Leonidus stayed outside. I wished they would have escorted me inside. I was pretty sure under different circumstances Pearl and I would have totally vibed.

"Have a seat, Ms. Kinsey," Balderdash said. He and his cohorts were sitting on top of the diner's counter, and their witches and warlocks stood behind them once again. "Any table is fine."

Becksy Ansel, a teenage witch, who waitressed at Lolo's brought me a cup of coffee, with two sugars and a small tub of French vanilla creamer. I smiled at her. She looked startled for a moment when she really looked at me. "I'm okay," I told her. "I just forgot to moisturize this morning. Thank you for the coffee. How's the pie today?"

"The apple is delicious," Becksy said. "I'll get you a slice."

I applauded the brave girl. She wasn't letting a group of intimidating cats intimidate her. She was currently dating Lincoln, Ford's younger brother. And when I say younger, I mean like twenty-years-apart younger. Since Becksy was a witch, Bryant had found a way to rationalize that his younger son dating outside his species was somehow my fault.

"How's Lincoln?" I asked.

Becksy blushed. "Good." She wiped her hands on her apron. "I'll be right back with the pie."

"Thanks." I turned my attention to the clowder, who were all looking at me like I'd grown another head. I guess they weren't used to have insolence served up to them in the form of me. "What can I do for you hairballs?"

A blur of pink-wrinkly skin knocked my coffee cup from the table.

"Damn it, Lonnie!" I hadn't added the cream and sugar yet, but the coffee was hot enough, that what splashed on my shirt burned. "Get away from me, you wrinkled monster."

"Have you looked at yourself in the mirror?" Lonnie thrust his chin in the air. "Pot meet kettle."

"Yeah, well, my wrinkles won't be permanent."

"If you don't accept me as your familiar, they will."

Queenie, with her sharp British accent, shouted, "Enough. I am unamused."

Doing my best Spike from the Buffy-verse impression, I said, "Well, I wouldn't want to do anything to get your knickers in a twist, love."

"Tell us where Lupitia and Tisiphone are hiding, Kinsey." This came from Jane the Tabby. "We don't want to punish you. It's not our way. We, familiars, are born for the sole purpose of partnership with a witch or warlock. Can't you see that what Tisiphone and Lupitia have done goes against our very nature? So much so, that it's never happened before."

Devi, the female Bombay added, "We can't allow this anomaly to exist in the world. It could potentially tear apart the fabric of magic itself."

"Seriously?" I asked, because, seriously, I wanted to know. What the black cat suggested seemed downright apocalyptic.

"Of course, we're serious," Balderdash said. "We

wouldn't have convened here in Paradise Falls if we weren't serious, you fatuous witch."

"Don't you dare body shame me!" I protested. Betsy took that moment to bring me a new cup of coffee and a big slice of pie.

"I didn't say you were fat, I said you fatuous, you know, silly and idiotic," Balderdash waved his paw in the air.

"I love my new curves," I told him. "Someone must have really hurt you for you to be so cruel." I knew what fatuous meant but riling these catholes up was a simple pleasure I couldn't resist.

"Never mind," he said with exasperation. "We don't have time for all this. Terrible things will happen if we don't break the familiar bond between Tisiphone and Lupitia."

"How do you know any of this is true? It sounds like a meta-episode for *Supernatural*, you know, the ones that offer comic relief from the Armageddon plot lines."

"This is not a television show," Deva shouted. He was getting pretty riled up. "This is real life, and you are playing a dangerous game."

"Just give me proof. Any proof that what you're saying is true. According to you, this has never happened before, so how do you know it will all end badly? Is there a prophecy ball sitting on a dusty shelf somewhere that I should know about?"

John, the male tabby said, "Jane's warlock, Larry, has seen it in a prophecy."

I glanced at the black-haired warlock behind Jane. His scathing gaze made me shiver.

"So, Larry." I took a bite of the apple pie in front of me, because, well, pie. Savored the flavor for a moment and swallowed. I pointed the fork at Larry. "You're a prophet. Give me an example of anything you've predicted coming true. Go ahead."

"How about the fall of the Roman empire? Is that good enough for you?" John said, vehemently defending his sister's warlock.

"Who didn't see that coming? I mean, really, once the Visigoths got on the scene, Rome was doomed." Thank you, History channel for that little documentary. I took a couple more bites of pie as the clowder watched on in sheer horror. When I was done, I stood up. "I am not your prisoner, and I'm done being interrogated. I'm out of here."

"You can't just leave," Queenie said.

"Watch me."

"Let her go," Balderdash told them. "For now."

Outside, I nodded to Pearl and flipped off Leonidus as I walked straight out of the parking lot and turned west up the sidewalk of Elysium toward Twelfth street. From there it was a couple of blocks to Valhalla, and my home away from home, aka the cop shop. I grabbed my phone from my purse and called the unknown number from the day before.

Ford picked up on the first ring. "Is everything okay?"

"I could ask you the same thing?" It was February and chillier out than I'd expected. The T-shirt and sweat pants would have been plenty warm if I still had my magic, but since I didn't… "I'm a couple of blocks from Lolo's heading toward the station on foot. Can you pick me up? It's pretty cold out, and I didn't bring a jacket."

"Where's your car?"

"At home with my jacket." I sighed. "The HFC enforcer came and got me. The cats wanted to corner me again to find out where Tiz and Skip-To-My-Lou are hiding. They were pretty adamant about wanting them both, which makes me wonder if they are behind the cat's disappearance. It doesn't seem likely."

"Did they hurt you?" I could hear the anger in his

voice, so I skipped the part about Leo dropping me on my knees.

"I'm fine. Just freezing. I didn't realize how many little things I used my magic for." I rubbed my upper arm with my free hand. "Like keeping warm." And dental hygiene. I wasn't sure if now was the time to reveal that I'd used Ford's toothbrush, though. "Can you come and get me?"

"I'm already on my way. I see you just ahead."

I looked up the street, and Ford's truck was less than a block away. Suddenly, I was self-conscious. Would my appearance shock him?"

He pulled up next to me, reached over and unlocked the passenger door. Being cold outweighed my vanity. I opened the door and climbed in, smoothing down my flyaway hair. "Hey," I said.

Ford, who's hair was suspiciously wet, put the car in Park. "Are you okay?"

"Did you just shower?" And since he hadn't been home, the better question was where had he showered. For the past couple of weeks, my guy had been acting secretive and covert.

"I don't know what you're talking about," he said. But

he ran his hand through his damp locks and gave me a sheepish look. "Honestly, Haze. I can't talk about it."

"It's not another woman?"

He gave me an exasperated look. "How could I be with another woman? You are my mate."

"I was," I said. "But now that I'm human..." My fluttering heart made me feel light headed, and I wanted to cry. Everything was so up in the air between the clowders investigation into Tizzy and my new fragile status.

A slight rumble emanating from Ford made me look up at him, but I couldn't keep the quiver out of my lower lip.

He reached over to me and pulled me into his arms. He tilted my chin and looked deeply into my eyes. His blue gaze melting my panties. "You are the most beautiful woman I've ever known, Hazel Kinsey. I thought that twenty years ago, I thought that last week, and I think that today. Don't ever doubt how much I love you, woman. Never."

"Even with the wrinkles and bruises?"

He nodded. "Yes, even with."

"Even without the vanilla and rum scent?"

A sexy smile tugged at his lips. "Even without the smell of teen spirit."

Tears crested my eyes. "I don't know what I did to deserve you, Ford." I shook my head. "Or maybe I'm your punishment. Were you bad in a past life?"

"If I was, I wouldn't change a thing. Whatever happens with this familiar business, we will be together. If that means moving away from Paradise Falls and going on the run with Tizzy, then that's what we'll do. I will love you until I take my last breath. I don't need a mate scent to tell me that you are the best part of my life."

I crawled up on his lap and straddled his thighs. I rose up on my knees and cradled Ford's face. I dipped my lips to his and kissed him. His hands slid under my T-shirt and up my back, his deft fingers unhooking my bra. He gently kneaded my spine in a way that felt good against the soreness as his tongue went all Conan the Conqueror with my mouth. Goddess, this man knew how to rev up my engine.

I squirmed against him, pleased when he moaned, his hard erection straining against his jeans. His hands wandered to the front of my body, his fingers slipping under the loose cups of my bra and caressing my ta-tas.

"Yes," I whispered against his mouth. I rocked

forward, mashing our bits together, the building tension in my body culminating in aching pleasure that begged to explode. "Yes, Ford. I'm going to—"

"Goddess, you two, it's broad daylight in a busy section of town!" Tizzy squeaked from the passenger seat. "I'm going to start wearing a blindfold before I show up."

Ford growled as he moved his hands from under my shirt. I slid into the middle area between him and the squirrel. "You have rotten timing," I told her.

A car honked behind us and I blushed. I'd been ready to have sex in the middle of a main street. Ack!

"You two need to get your priorities straight," she chastised. "Have you heard anything about Lupitia? She could be hurt, Hazel. They could be torturing her for information about me. Have you thought about that while you're bumping uglies like two horny dingoes?"

I flushed guiltily.

"We never actually got to the ugly bumping yet, thanks to you," Ford said.

"I will squeeze your belly if I want you to say something, Teddy Ruxpin."

"Stop it," I said. "Both of you."

My phone rang, saving me from having to say more. It was Tanya. "Hey," I said. "I'm putting you on speaker-phone. I have Ford and Tiz with me."

"Bryant and I have been scouring the rules, and we can't find anything specific about a familiar bonding with a familiar, but he thinks they are using some of the rules with broader language to charge Tizzy and Lupitia. There is also a directive that if a familiar's witch bond is broken, they are to turn themselves over to the high clowder for reassignment. If Tizzy didn't know Lupitia's witch died, you have a strong case to save her, but Lupitia wouldn't have any defense. She would have known the instant it happened."

"Crap," I mouthed to Tiz. "Okay. Is there anything else that might be useful?"

"I've called around to some contacts in other para-normal communities. No one has ever heard of a familiar bonding with another familiar. It really is virgin territory. This case may set a precedent."

"Ceasar's nuts! I'm not trying to be the next Roe versus Wade," Tizzy said. "I don't want to make history. I just want to live a quiet life with Hazel and Lupitia. I don't even care about the extra power. I'd happily return it all, go magic free, if I could just get my life back."

"I'm sorry, Tisiphone," Tanya said. "I wish we had better news."

After she hung up, I looked at Ford. "Romy Quinn died in witch jail. Maybe the way she died could shed some light on how this familiar-familiar bond happened."

"She killed herself, Haze. There isn't anything mystical about suicide," Tizzy said.

"No, but maybe if we knew how she killed herself, that might help." I scrolled through the contacts on my phone until I found WIC, which stood for "Witch In Charge" and hit the call button.

My grandmother picked up on the first ring. "Hello, Hazel. What can I do for you?"

CHAPTER 8

C lementine Battles appeared in my house at noon. She wore a white cashmere power suit with a flared leg and a heeled boot that matched. Her silver hair was pinned tightly into her signature bun, completing the look of authority and severity she liked to display.

"Hi, Grandma," I said, as she made a file appear out of thin air.

"I have the information about Romy Quinn you wanted." She handed me the manila folder without ceremony, an act that made me suspicious. "But, you do know you'll owe me a favor for this right?"

And there it was. I was going to be owing the old Battle-axe favors until I was four-hundred years old if my life kept throwing twists at me every time I turned around. This was the third time I'd called on the All-Powerful Inquisitor for help. Her efforts were hardly ever direct, though. She seemed to abide by the view that the Goddess helps those who help themselves. But she was good at pointing me in the right direction. And, she'd helped me find Lily's uncle in Moonrise, Missouri. That was a favor I wasn't sure I could ever repay.

"Deal," I told her. "If I don't get my magic back, though, I'm not sure how I'll be able to return the favor in any meaningful way."

"You know people in the human world. Important government people. Those kinds of contacts can be useful. Being a witch is not all about magic."

"Tell that to my sagging boobs," I told her.

"You have aged beautifully, Hazel. You should embrace the fact that by human standards, you're gorgeous."

I didn't say it out loud, but I appreciated her compliment. If I had to live as a human, I could do with some confidence. At least for a few years, maybe even a few decades.

Then I would eventually get really old and decrepit and die. Or maybe get one of those awful human diseases and die sooner rather than later.

And...I was depressed again. "So how did Romy kill herself?"

"Sheer determination," Clementine said. "Romy's death was unique. I've never had a witch kill herself while in my custody. She used a pencil."

I blinked. "She what?"

"She had pencils and paper to write letters or to journal. We encourage that sort of thing as part of their self-reflection. She sharpened one of the pencils then put the pointed end inside her ear canal, put the eraser end against the wall and..." My grandmother moved her head sideways, demonstrating Romy's self-impalement.

"That's determined. And graphic. Ouch." I rubbed my ear.

"No kidding." She tapped her deep, red lower lip. "Surprisingly, there wasn't a lot of blood. Really, if it hadn't been for the two inches of pencil sticking out of her ear, we might have struggled to find a cause of death."

"I'm not sure if that helps any but thank you. It would have been nice if her death could have explained any of this crazy mess, but it sounds like she was just desperate to die."

"You know, strangely, there was a second suicide a month later. A Roberta Mendell. She'd been in the Salem jail for fifteen years for turning a human landlord into a dung beetle so he could find out what it was like to have to 'live in a shit house.' Her words, not mine."

"From San Francisco area?"

"Yes," said Clementine. "How can you possibly know that?"

"An FBI pal of mine worked the missing persons case. He said the guy showed up claiming to have been turned into a bug by his witch tenant. We'd gotten a good laugh out of that one. Really, I thought it was just another case of someone taking bad acid. I can't believe it was true." I chuckled.

"Easy to laugh when you aren't the one digging through porcine feces to find the sleazy buffoon."

I gave her a pointed, incredulous look that I hoped conveyed the sentiment, *No way, Jose.* "You dug through pig poop?"

"No, of course not, but my investigators did, and Roberta was due to get paroled next year. After she had taken her life, in a very similar way to Romy, I had to add extra wards to the cells to make sure it didn't happen again."

"One more favor," I said. "Do you think you can get my magic back? I never realized how crappy getting old must feel. I can't tell you how many ways I used to razz my old boss back in Kansas City."

"Sorry." She shook her head. "I can't interfere with the High Familiar Clowder. It's part of the Witch-Familiar agreement. If I piss them off, they may just walk away from us, but I do know how to keep my mouth shut." She put her finger to her lips. "I won't tell them that you are hiding Tisiphone behind the couch."

My eyes widened. She'd known Tiz was in the room the whole time, and she hadn't let on once. And while she might not take on the clowder for me, it looked like she wouldn't help them either. It was the best I could hope for. "Thanks, Grandma."

She winked and leaned forward so I could kiss her cheek then poofed out. Tizzy came around the couch and scampered over to me. "The old Battle-axe is one scary witch."

"You're telling me." But at least I got what my grandmother had promised. Fat lot of good it did me.

"I've come to give you an update," my father said, suddenly behind me.

I yelped as I spun around on him. "Don't startle me like that."

"I'm sorry." He looked chagrinned. "Mike Crandall says that the clowder has seven rooms at the Paradise Falls Inn. Each familiar with his or her respective warlock or witch has their own rooms. Balderdash's and Pluto's warlock and witch are having an affair, but the weremongoose on Pluto's room said they didn't talk about Tiz's case. Queenie and her witch disapparated for half an hour. No idea where they went. John and Jane have been napping, but Jane's warlock was on the phone with a family member. Something about the death of someone close."

"And Deva and Devi?"

Dad shook his head. "Nothing there either."

Tizzy climbed up to my shoulder. "So no chatter about Lupitia? I know they have to have her. She wouldn't just leave me."

"I believe you, Tiz." I scratched her cheek. "But I don't think the clowder has her, but we won't give up until we find her. I promise."

"Mary Lowe says her trackers are picking up a lot of false trails in the woods, but she's not giving up either." He thinned his lips. "I wish I had better news."

"Me too, but I appreciate all your efforts. Thanks, Dad."

He gave me a quick kiss on the forehead and popped out again. I'd never been a fan of translocation spelling, but at this point, I longed for any magic. Even magic that might put me in the middle of a mountain. Since I was never very good with witchcraft, the mountain had been a real possibility. Once I'd ended up in the ocean. Luckily, I'd been near the shore, or it could have been disastrous.

"Fifty-two hours and counting, Tiz. What should we tackle next?"

"Lunch," she said without missing a beat.

My stomach growled its agreement. "Lunch it is."

THE NEW CHINESE RESTAURANT IN TOWN, RUN BY A family of werefoxes, also delivered. In forty-five minutes, the food arrived. The smell of moo shu pork and cashew chicken, minus the chicken for Tiz, made my mouth water. We'd also ordered some orange rolls, which weren't exactly Chinese, more refrigerator cinnamon rolls deep fried and topped with orange glaze. Delicious.

Do You Believe In Magic played when I got my first big mouthful of moo shu. I let out a muffled *argh!*, chewing as fast as my jaw would allow. I swallowed the sweet and savory bite, finally. "Stay out of sight," I told Tiz.

She grabbed three cashews from her plate and went to hide behind the couch.

The doorbell went off again before I could reach the front of the house. I put my finger on my eyelid and tried to control a newly formed twitch with my right hand, while I opened the door with my left. "What?"

On the porch, Platinum Pearl and her fluffy sidekick aka "the Enforcer" waited for me.

"Pluto would like to see you in private," Pearl said. "We were asked to invite you to his motel room for a friendly conversation."

Pluto was the Siamese cat. The one that had laughed at my joke. "Is this another order? A summons?"

"No," Leonidus said. "It is a request."

"What room is he in?"

"Number twenty-three," Pearl said. "We can give you a ride."

"No thanks. I'll drive myself." Besides, I didn't want to get stuck in town again with no vehicle. "I'm in the middle of lunch, and I plan to finish. Just tell Pluto I'll be there in the next two hours."

Pearl gave me a two-finger salute, and she and the warrior marshmallow walked back out to her sports car. I watched them until they roared off down the driveway.

"They're gone," I yelled to Tiz. She didn't answer. I walked into the living room. "Tiz?" Still no answer. I went to the kitchen. Her plate sat on the center island, but no sign of her. "Tiz?"

I went back to the living room and to the couch. "They're gone. You can come out now." I looked behind the couch. The only thing I found was two cashews and tiny claw marks etched into the hardwood around them. My heart fluttered, and my breath quickened. "Tizzy!" I shouted.

She was gone. Pearl and Leonidus had tricked me. They were the distraction while someone snatched my Tiz. I gathered in my will, drawing on the air around me to power a magic spell that would send them all to a hell in which there would be no return, then heaved a sobbing exhalation when I felt nothing. I took a second to mourn my magic because a second was all I could afford. Tizzy was in trouble, and I wouldn't let her down by wallowing in despair.

I grabbed my purse, my keys, and my phone and raced to my vehicle. I hit the mic button on my phone after I started the car and said, "Call everyone!"

CHAPTER 9

FORD, MY DAD, and Tanya met me at the Paradise Falls Inn. I dashed up the stairs, feeling slower than molasses with each step.

Ford banged on the door to room twenty-three.

"Open up, Pluto. Now," he boomed. And then without waiting, my man kicked the door in with a ferocity that made my heart leap.

Inside, an astonished Siamese and his warlock, the one with the blond hair, stared at us, their mouths agape.

The warlock, who'd been reading *Twenty Shades of Blue* in bed, squawked, "What is the meaning of this?"

Pluto jumped up on the bed next to his warlock. "Can we help you, Ms. Kinsey?" He looked at Ford, my dad, and Tanya, and added, "And family."

I didn't correct him that Tanya wasn't my family, because, well, she was here, and that meant something to me. "Where's Tizzy?" I demanded.

The cat tilted his head. "That's what we want to know. If we had her, we wouldn't still be in this lovely town." He made the word "lovely" sound like "Goddess-forsaken." "Believe me when I say, I would love for this to be all over. But first, we require both Tisiphone and Lupitia. We have neither, Ms. Kinsey, I assure you."

"And I'm going to assure my foot right up your furry butthole," I told him. "I might not have my magic, but over fifteen years in law enforcement has taught me all I need to know to kick your ass ten ways to Sunday."

"You have some nerve," the warlock said, but he pulled up the covers around his chest as a way to put a barrier between me and him. "Get out of our room."

"It's okay, Gwyn. Ms. Kinsey isn't going to resort to violence." Pluto gave me a direct look. "I have not taken your familiar but tell me why you think I have."

"Because your cretins came to my home and told me you wanted to talk to me alone, and after they left, Tiz was gone."

"So you've been lying about being in contact with Tisiphone."

"Yes," I blurted out. "But so not the point, Mr. Pointy."

"Pluto is fine." He walked to the edge of the bed. "Who are these cretins you speak of?"

"Pearl and pocket-sized merengue."

The warlock stifled a giggle.

I glared at him.

"Sorry," Gwyn said. "I laughed when I'm nervous. Besides, it was funny."

"I'm not doing a standup routine here. I want Tiz back. Now!"

Ford let a roar rip that shook the walls in the room. I didn't have to look at him to know he'd shifted into his partial form, because the big and fearful eyes of both Pluto and Gwyn, told me just how big, furry, and scary my boo looked right now.

My dad and Tanya began to chant. Even with no magic of my own, I could feel their current of power on the air.

"Enough," Pluto said. "I promise you, I sent no one to your home, Hazel."

He'd used my first name. A technique I'd put to practice many a time when talking a suspect down from the ledge.

"This doesn't have to get ugly," he added. "Tell me what Pearl and Leonidus said."

"Just what I told you, that you wanted to meet with me away from the group. One on one. *Gato y mano.* And then, you all kidnapped Tizzy." I held my breath for a second to keep from crying. What if she was already beyond my reach? What if they had decommissioned her or something? Did they decommission familiars? Would she just disappear forever? I couldn't bear to think of a world without my girl in it. "There was a struggle," I told Pluto. "She…"

My father stepped forward. "My daughter had until tomorrow to turn Tisiphone and Lupitia in. By going to her house and forcing the issue, you've crossed a line."

"I didn't ask Pearl or Leo to request a private audience with you."

"Liar!"

"What would make you believe the truth? I'm happy to take a lie detector if you have one handy."

A lie detector was exactly what I needed. I pulled out my phone and hit the second button in my top five. When the soft voice of my BFF Lily Mason answered, I nearly started crying again.

"Haze? Are you there? Are you okay?" Lily asked. A

loud racket of cages rattling and barking dogs made it hard to hear her.

My lower lip quivered. "Are you alone?" I knew she worked most days at the rescue shelter for pit bull breeds that she ran with her friend Parker Knowles. I'd never met him, but Lily told me that she cared for him beyond platonic.

"I can be." I heard her shut a door and the barking became muffled. "I am now."

"Tizzy's been familiar-napped!" I took a deep breath. "I'm sorry. I'm trying to keep it together."

"What do you mean? What's familiar-napped? Is she in some kind of magical sleep and you can't wake her up?"

"No." I wiped my nose with a tissue Tanya handed to me. "She's been taken. I'm so scared for her."

"What do you need from me?" Lily's voice was calm, and it helped ground me. "Whatever it is, you've got it."

During the fiasco at Halloween, we found out Lily, who was a werecougar, had a witch in the family shed. Her great-grandmother on her mother's side had been a truth-dealer. The witch's power forced the people around her to speak only the truth. While Lily's power, which had been latent until the rogue coven opened the hellmouth, wasn't as potent as her ancestors, but still, it made people want to tell her the truth, and when someone lied, she would feel it in her bones like a vibration. In other words, she was a walking, talking lie detector.

"Is it okay if Dad pops in to get you?" I asked her.

"Of course." Now she sounded worried, too. "Can you tell me for how long?"

"Long enough to get to the truth."

"Give me ten minutes to tell Parker I need to take the afternoon off. These dogs need someone here, and I'm the only one in the shelter right now. Don't worry, though, he'll cover the rest of my shift."

I looked at Pluto and Gwyn. They both looked way too calm for my taste. I needed to shake them up. "Can you bring Smooshie along? I have a cat for her to play with."

I could hear the smile in Lily's voice. "You got it. Give me ten minutes, and I will text you with my location."

When I hung up, Pluto asked, "What's a Smooshie?"

I smiled at the Siamese. "You're about to find out."

Fifteen minutes later, my dad came back with Lily. At

five feet tall and probably not much more than one hundred pounds, she packed a lot of friendship in her diminutive self. Her long, thick cinnamon colored hair was pulled back in a ponytail.

"Hazel," she said, embracing me. She took in my new aged look. "What happened? Who beat the crap out of you?"

"The floor," I told her. "I'm human." Before she could ask, I added, "I don't have time to explain, but I promise when this is all over, I'll tell you everything."

She nodded.

"What is that thing!" Gwyn jumped to his feet on the bed and backed against the headboard.

I smiled as I took in the ninety-pound mass of hard muscle covered in red and white fur, and a tongue that hung inches past her chin at the end of a short leash my BFF held in her hand. The pit bull's butt wiggled with excitement as her deadly tail whacked the hell out of my dad's leg.

I looked at the petrified Pluto and his warlock and grinned. "That would be Smooshie."

Pluto stood up on the toes of all four of his paws, his back arched, his hackles stacked like dominoes and hissed in the mammoth dog's direction.

"If you lie to me about Tizzy," I told him. "I'm feeding you to the dog."

WE'D BEEN AT THE QUESTIONS FOR HALF AN HOUR, and we hadn't gathered any more information than we had before. My time was ticking away, and without magic, I couldn't feel Tiz. I didn't know if she was scared or hurt or, even worse, dead.

"I'm sorry," Lily said. "The cat is telling the truth. He doesn't know where Tizzy is, and he has no idea who took her. Neither does his warlock."

"I think it's time we had a talk with the entire High Familiar Clowder," my dad said. "Someone sent the enforcers to your home, or they acted on their own for some other purpose. Either way, we need to find out."

Pluto, who continued to give Smooshie a weary look, but was no longer in a defensive posture, said, "I agree."

I raised a questioning brow.

"I told you that I didn't have anything to do with Tisiphone's disappearance. And frankly, I'm not sure the clowder is in the right in this situation," he said. "I'm not the only one to think this, but we vote by committee, and majority rules."

I thought about the Shifter-Witch Coalition. Most democracies ran that way. "Can you call for an emergency meeting with the clowder?"

"They will need a reason to convene so quickly."

"Tell them I'm ready to talk. I'm ready to tell them where Tiz is located and turn her in so I can get my magic back." I put my hands on my hips. "That should get their attention." And hopefully, it would throw off whoever was responsible for taking her, because at least one of those bastards would know I was lying, and maybe they would do or say something that would give themselves away.

THE CLOWDER SET THE MEETING TIME FOR SEVEN IN the evening. So much for urgency. Five hours was too long to stew in my misery. Lily checked in with Parker and her uncle. I really was happy for her. She'd found a place where she finally felt like she belonged. I just wished I didn't miss her so much.

My father had called on the coalition to come to the house at five-thirty for dinner and a strategy meeting. Robert Pierce and Mike Crandell were the last to arrive. Mike had a friend with him. The man was lanky in a way that brought the classic Ichabod Crane to mind. His brown hair was cut just above his ears and combed neatly with a side part. His narrow face and sharp eyes reflected a quick intelligence.

Mike presented the new man to the group. "This is Patrick Edger. He's been keeping an eye on the familiars since last night. I thought you might want a report directly from him."

"Oh, the weremongoose," I said. I extended my hand. "Thanks for the help, Patrick."

He nodded. "Yes, ma'am."

"Do you have anything useful?"

"Maybe." He pursed his lips. "Those witches, warlocks, and familiars are boring bunch. A lot of conversations about *Real Housewives* and *Teen Moms*. They do way too much binge-watching of reality television. I thought my time would be a complete bust, but I overheard a man and a woman talking about how this time they would make it work. That they would figure it out, and since the witch's magic had been cut, they didn't even need to kill this time."

I gulped. "They mean me. Since my power is gone, they don't need to kill me."

"I'm assuming," Patrick said. "Then the woman said they knew Tisiphone was at the house with you, and that all they had to do was create a little misdirection to nab her."

My stomach lurched. "Who was it?"

"I spent a lot of time in the air vents listening, but I couldn't see." He shook his head. "I'm sorry."

"No British accents?" I asked.

"Not in that room."

"That rules out Queenie." I paced the living room. "Can you identify the witch if you heard her voice again?"

"Or familiar," my father added.

Patrick nodded. "I can."

"It has to be Balderdash," I said. "He acts like someone hellbent on world domination."

"We shouldn't jump to conclusions," my dad said. "We'll no more when we get them all in the same room tonight."

I sighed. "I'm so tired." I looked at Lily. "How do humans live in such frail bodies?"

She shook her head. "They're amazing creatures. Tough and resilient because they have to be."

Every part of me ached, from my back where the door had thrown chunks, to the bruise on my right cheek where my face had hit the hardwood, and my knees. Mother Nature and all four of her seasons, my knees hadn't been the same since Pee Wee Puffball had slammed me down on them. In the past two days, the teacup Persian had really worked me over.

Tanya strolled over to me, her heeled boots striking the floor hard with each step. She put her hand on my shoulders and mouthed an incantation I couldn't make out. When she finished, my aches and pains were gone, and my energy was renewed.

"There," she said brightly. "Better?"

"Thanks, Doc," I said and gave her a grateful smile. "I feel much better."

"I'm glad I could help," she said. "I rarely get to use my healing spells since shifters, witches, and warlocks hardly ever need a doctor. It's why I became a medical examiner. It's the only lucrative career choice for a doctor in a paranormal town." She beamed when my dad took her hand. "Anyhow," Tanya said. "I didn't know if it would work on you since you're human now. I'm glad it did."

"Me too." And I really was glad, but I hated to be beholden to Tanya. Now I owed her a favor as well. Then I gave her a sharp look as it dawned on me that she could have healed my aches and pains much sooner if she'd wanted. "How come you did this now? Not earlier?"

"Earlier I was angry with you for the mean comments. Now, I'm not."

"Fair enough." I nodded my respect. "Okay. Let's eat and get this show on the road."

CHAPTER 10

THE MEETING WAS set at the coalition building on Heavenly Street, just down from the department of motor vehicles. It was almost seven o'clock now. The coalition went ahead of me to set up the room, and my dad texted when the HFC arrived.

"All present and accounted for, according to Dad," I told Ford and Lily. "Are we ready."

Smooshie had pushed her big head up front between Ford and I. She kept licking his arms and neck, much to his annoyance.

"Does she smell like vanilla and rum?" I winked at him.

"Smart ass," he replied.

"Smoosh." Lily hooked her fingers in the massive

dog's collar. "Stop flirting with the bear shifter." She giggled.

I giggled. For that split second, everything was right with the world. Only it wasn't. How could I laugh when Tiz was Goddess-knows-where? Whoever took her already killed a witch. I wish we knew who'd been murdered, but Patrick hadn't heard any names.

Speaking of the weremongoose. "I hope Patrick can identify the voices. I hate feeling so helpless."

"You are the toughest chick I know, Haze Kinsey," Lily said. Which was nice of her to say, but I was one hundred and twenty percent certain Lily held the toughest chick title. She'd been through so much, and the fact that she could function day to day was a testament to her resilience.

"Ditto that," Ford added. "You got this, babe."

I grabbed both their hands. "We got this." A long pink tongue swiped my ear. I reached back and scratched Smooshie's neck. "All of us."

I FELT EERILY CALM AS I WALKED INTO THE COALITION. Patrick the weremongoose stood by the door as we entered. My dad and the other members of the Shifter-

Witch council each sat in their chairs on the small stage. A show of dominance. Much like the one the HFC had put on for me in our first meeting. Someone had placed folding chairs in front of the ceremonial altar. A nice touch. I'd lay money on it being Bryant's idea. He knew how to make a show of being in charge.

To my surprise, all the witches and warlocks had sat in them, each stroking their cats, which conjured visions of cartoon villains plotting in their evil lairs. I expected one of them, at any second, to steeple his or her hands, and say, "I will blow up the world in sixty seconds if you don't comply with my demands."

I strolled in front of them with the confidence of someone in law enforcement for half her life.

"Can we get on with this?" Queenie asked. "The sooner you give up Tisiphone, the sooner I can get out of this hovel of a village."

There was a murmur of agreement from several of the HFC. I crossed my arms and stared them down. All of them but Pluto and Gwyn looked away when my gaze snapped on them. I nodded to Lily, who'd been waiting in the front for my signal. She was led in to the room by Smooshie, whose excitement for the new place and all the wonderfully small creatures, had her yanking at her leash.

She barked, her yips high and delighted as they neared the clowder.

"What is that monster doing in here?" John the tabby shouted. "I demand an explanation."

"The only monsters in this room are sitting in cold metal chairs," I snapped. "One of you took Tisiphone and Lupitia, and I'm going to suss you out now. Tonight." I shook my fist at the group. "And then I'm going to make you pay."

Balderdash laughed. "You and what army, Ms. Kinsey? Have you forgotten you are one of the forsaken right now. Do you really think you can demand anything from us?"

"What do you mean when you say one of us took the fugitive familiars?" Devi asked. "This is simply not true."

I looked at Lily.

"She's telling the truth. She believes what she's saying."

I held up my hands. I addressed the guilty directly. They would know who they were. "Two down, five to go. And when I find you, you familiar-napping, witch-killing bastards, you better believe that it won't just be me you'll be facing."

Deva's witch blanched.

"Is it you?" I pointed at the male Bombay cat. "Speak."

"You are out of your mind," he said. "I thought we were here so you could turn over Tisiphone."

Lily nodded. "Truth."

"Three down," I told them, addressing John, Jane, Balderdash, and Queenie. "And when I find you, I'm going to let Smooshie here eat you."

Smooshie, upon hearing her name, gave a playful growl and bark that sounded menacing as hell. The effect it had on the remaining familiars was brilliant.

"I'm not going to sit here and be interrogated by a worthless human," Jane said. "Larry, it's time for us to go."

Her warlock stood up, cradling the female tabby in his arms.

"That's her," Patrick said. "That's the voice I heard. The one that murdered the witch and planned Tizzy's abduction."

"I did no such thing," Jane denied.

"Liar," Lily pointed. "What have you done with Tizzy?" Lily's eyes flashed bright green as her cougar surfaced. She made a noise of anger that sent shivers over my skin. Smooshie started barking in earnest now, trying to jump at Jane and Larry.

"This isn't true," John said. "It can't be. Tell them, sister."

"You never did have any vision for the future," Jane said. "Such a disappointment." She turned her head to look at Larry. "Grab her."

Larry reached out and snatched my wrist. Suddenly, everything seemed to travel in slow motion. Ford furred out, my dad, Robert Pierce, and Tanya began chanting, Mary Lowe was already on four legs, a large deadly cougar ready to pounce. Smooshie tore at Larry's leg, and then just as suddenly, I was somewhere else.

Larry shoved me to the ground, the cold concrete cut into the palm of my hands.

"Haze!" Tizzy shouted. She was in a small cage laced with rune stones and wards. In another cage, Lupitia lay still and quiet. I prayed to the Goddess she wasn't dead.

"What do you want with them?" I seethed with anger, the rage making me strong. "How do you think you can possibly get away with this?"

"I hoped to do it with as little fuss as possible. You

were supposed to turn over Tisiphone and Lupitia, take Lonnie as your new familiar, we'd come back in a month and kill you, and take Lonnie back."

I got up and dusted my hands on my sweatpants. "Lonnie? What does that hairless mongrel have to do with any of this?"

"Lonnie," Jane said a touch too dramatically, "is my lover."

I threw up a little in my mouth. "Yuck. He looks like a fully formed embryo."

"Shut up, you insolent woman," Lonnie said as he came out from behind a box in the corner of the concrete dungeon Larry had popped us into.

"Where are we?" If felt like a cellar or a basement. Cold and damp. No windows. All gray concrete.

"Hazel, they killed Lonnie's witch, trying to copy what happened between Lupitia and me. They want to get the same power boost."

"Uh oh," Larry said. "Spoiler alert." He kicked Tizzy's cage. "Shut up, rat, or I'll shut you up permanently."

"Just tell us how you three did it," Jane said. "If you do, I'll let you go."

"No, you won't."

"You're right." They cat flicked out her claws. "No, I won't. But I might let you live."

There was a stack of boxes in the corner of the room, some simple tools, screwdrivers, a small hammer, pliers, and such, hanging on a hook and peg board. One of the boxes read, *Personal Effects: Roberta Mendell.*

"The other suicide," I said. The one my grandmother had told me about. Lonnie had belonged to Roberta. "Traitor." I pointed at the wrinkled monster with the big ears. "How could you let them kill your witch, Lonnie?"

"She deserted me," he said. "So, I made my own family. After a while, I didn't need or want her anymore. I want to belong to Jane and Larry. Tell us how you did it."

"Very clever, Kinsey," Jane said. "You are smarter than you look. Of course, you don't look very bright, so you're far from a genius."

Crap, if we were at Roberta Mendell's place, it meant we were in San Francisco. How in the world was I going to get rescued in California?

Larry smiled. "I guess you've figured out you're no longer in Paradise Falls. There is no one here to help you. And without mine and Jane's help, you can never be restored as a witch. That means, you will die alone down here, and no one will ever find you. Not even to bury your bones."

Tizzy shook her cage. "If you hurt, Hazel, I swear I'll pulverize your nuts, Larry. You'll be singing soprano. Until I explode your head."

"Shut up, Tisiphone," Jane said. "You are in no position to make demands." The tabby stretched her tail up high. "I, on the other hand, have all the leverage. You will tell me what I want to know, or I will kill your ex-witch."

"Don't!" Tizzy screamed.

While Jane and Tizzy had exchanged threats, I'd inched my way toward the wall of boxes.

"I've had enough of your mouth," Jane said. "Larry, show her the virtue of silence."

Larry's hand shot into the cage, and he grabbed Tizzy by the throat.

"Hey!" I shouted. Jane, Larry, and Lonnie all focused their attention on me. The seemed surprised to see me standing next to the wall of tools. "No one grabs my squirrel." I gripped the screwdriver in my hand. "No one."

Larry's mouth dropped open, and he began to laugh. Jane and Lonnie joined in. "Stupid Hazel. Do you really think you can attack me before I stop you? I have the power here. The magic. Not you." He winked. "I bet you wish you had your gun about now."

I smirked and shook my head. "You're the idiot if you think the only thing they taught me at Quantico was how to shoot a gun." My shoulder felt a little stiff, but I didn't hesitate. I flipped the screwdriver around to the metal point and fired it at Larry. The Phillip's head pierced his eyeball all the way to the hilt.

He reached up, disbelief in his eye that didn't have a screwdriver in it. "I...I...I..."

"You die," I said helpfully. "That's what you do."

He toppled over.

"Larry!" Jane screeched. "You've ruined everything. Everything!"

I picked her and Lonnie up by the scruffs of their necks. "Without Larry, you guys have no magic. You see, that's a witch thing." Unfortunately, without Larry, I'd never get my power back either. He'd been a part of creating the spell to strip me of my magic, and it would have required all of the clowder to return it back to me.

"I can't feel him," Jane cried. "He's gone. He's gone."

Lonnie struggled under my grip. "This was all Jane's idea. They coerced me, her and Larry."

"How can you betray me, Lonnie? I thought you loved me."

"I never loved you," he said. "I wanted the power same as you."

"While you two lovebirds work it out, I'll just be getting my familiar and going now. I shoved the two cats into an empty packing box and rushed toward the metal cages covered in runes.

Jane started to laugh. "You can't get into her cage. It's warded against all magical creatures," Jane said with venom. "One touch and the wards will fry your brain. Only I can break the runes, and if you don't let me go, Tizzy will never be free. And since this room is locked from the outside, this concrete hole will be the last place you ever see alive, witch!"

I raised a finger. "Only, as you've been so fond to point out, I'm not currently a witch, am I?" And I hoped my new status held up to the rules of the runes, because while the clowder may have taken my magic, I'd been born witch, so it was a toss up.

I cautiously reached down and grazed the lid with my fingertips. It was cold, but I didn't feel even the slightest tingle. "Hah!" I stuck my tongue out at Jane as I lifted the lid on Tiz's then Lupitia's cages.

With the warding broken, Tizzy blinked herself out of

her little prison and into Lupitia's. I heard her say, "It's okay. I'm here, Lulu. I'm here. It's going to be okay."

"Is she?" I asked.

Tizzy shook her head. "She's hurt, but alive." I could hear the pain in Tiz's voice.

Luputia placed a paw on Tizzy's face. "You saved me, my love," she told Tiz.

Technically, I'd saved the both of them, and without any magic, I might add, but I wasn't going to ruin their moment. I stomped over the Jane and Lonnie and picked them up by the scruff of the neck. I pointed them in Tiz's direction. "You know why you couldn't make it work? There it is, plain as the nose on your face. Those two weren't trying to be more powerful. They were just trying to stay together." In other words, love. Real and true. That had been the key. The one thing Jane and Lonnie never possessed.

I lifted the lid off of Tiz's cage and dropped the two of them in. "You can think about that until they send you to the between."

I looked at Tiz. "Do you have enough magic to blink us out of here?"

"I can try," she said. "But I doubt it. I tried once with Lupitia and I didn't have enough power for that."

I put my hand on her back as she held her love and closed her eyes. Nothing happened.

She shook her head. "I can't."

"What about yourself?" I asked. "Go home and get my dad to come and take us all back."

She closed her eyes, but nothing happened again.

Jane, who really was beginning to get on my last nerve, laughed once more. "This room is magically sealed. Only Larry could apparate in and out. You are so screwed!"

"And so are you," I said.

"I don't even care anymore," Jane said. "I'll gladly watch all of you rot." She swiped her open claws at Lonnie, leaving dark trails of blood in five lines on his grossly pink skin.

"Get her away from me!" he said.

I ran upstairs and tried the door. Sure enough, it was made of steel and there was no handle on this side. Larry had bolted the door on the outside to prevent any chance of escape. I kicked it, feeling the shock as it jolted up my let to my knee.

"Ow." I trudged down the stair. "I'm sorry Tiz. I don't know how to get us out of here."

"Jane has to know how to break Larry's magical wards. Let me stick my fingers in her brains and dig around for the information," Tizzy said. She wiggled her claws for emphasis.

"And why do you think that will work?" I asked her.

She shrugged. "I saw it in a movie. It worked for the cyborgs. I don't know why it wouldn't work for me." She blew on her nails.

Jane's eyes widened, and Lonnie's skin blanched to a ghostly white.

"You wouldn't dare," Jane said.

Tizzy chittered. "I'm due some payback." She gave Lupitia a kiss between her ears then started toward the cage. "I'll flip a cat to see who I probe first."

"Larry," Jane said abruptly.

"Larry's dead," I said, toeing the corpse's foot just to make sure he didn't pop up and start exploding stuff.

"No, stupid." Jane rolled her eyes at me. "He has a phone. You can call for help."

"Oh." Now, I did kind of feel stupid. It hadn't even occurred to me to check.

I patted down Larry's jacket pockets until I found his cell phone. I could only remember my own number.

Technology made using contacts way too convenient, so I dialed myself, and hoped that someone had grabbed my purse from the coalition.

"Hello," Ford said. "Who is this?"

"It's me," I said.

"Where are you?" His voice was strained. "I've been tearing Paradise Falls apart trying to find you."

"I'm in San Francisco. Can you send my dad for me?"

CHAPTER 11

THE HFC APOLOGIZED for not being able to make me a witch again. I knew what would happen if I killed Larry, but it was worth it. That jerk put his hands on my Tiz. No one did that. Ever. The clowder ruled again on Tizzy's case, once they had all the information about Jane, and in a five to one vote, the one being Queenie—what a jerk—they allowed Tiz to remain my familiar. Of course, they didn't allow Lupitia to remain hers. Instead, they compromised with us. They broke the familiar bond between them, and my dad agreed to be Lupitia's warlock. That way Tizzy and Lupitia would never have to part. It also meant, no more witch magic for my squirrel. She didn't seem to mind one bit.

Before my father returned Lily back to Moonrise, my bestie confided in me about her attraction to the human she worked for, Parker Knowles, and how she'd accidentally revealed her cougar self to him. I offered to have my dad put a forgetting spell on him, but Lily was a hard "no" on that option. I think she is really falling for him, which makes me sad for her in so many ways. Shifters didn't mate with humans, so while she might eventually be with him, they could never truly be together.

Even though I wanted to believe that it could be different with Ford and I, I was feeling fatalistic. Especially since Ford was still being cagey and secretive. And, while I didn't really believe he would cheat on me, I needed to know what he was getting up to when he disappeared. Following him wasn't too difficult, even without magic. I'd spent many years in the FBI tracking suspects at a distance, and this suspect was driving like he didn't care if anyone was following him.

I wore a baseball cap and sunglasses and used one of my deputies' cars just in case he checked his rearview mirror and let other cars in front of me when I could and still track him. Once he turned onto Paradise Falls Lake road, I knew he could only be going to one destination, so I drove past and waited five minutes before driving a half mile down the drive and parked on the side of the road. The walking distance to the lake was only another half mile, and I stayed inside the wooded tree line to provide cover as I approached the lake.

The roar of laughter along with the snarls and growls of what sounded like a mob of men made me put a little speed in my step. What the heck was Ford up to? And why did he have an audience?

My hands hurt where they'd scraped on the dried bark of a tree, and the scratches didn't immediately heal like they normally would. I rubbed them together to ward off the winter chill and shoved my hands into my jacket pocket. The fact that I needed gloves to keep warm drove home the fact that I was human. Mortal. And in the human world, I was moving into middle age. I couldn't force Ford into a life where he would have to watch me shrivel up and die. Besides, without the mate scent, I'd never be able to give him children. I knew how much he wanted a family of his own.

Splashing, coughing, followed by a recognizable bear roar snapped me out of my pity party. Ford was in trouble! I ran, ignoring the ache in my ankles and knees.

Seriously, if I was going to stay human, I had to start exercising.

When I could see the end of the woods and a hint of lake, instead of gracefully bursting on the scene, I tripped over a downed tree and screamed as I tumbled out into the open, hitting my head on a rock as I fell to the hard ground. When I raised myself from the dried grass, I saw twenty dripping wet men standing naked at the water's shore. One of them was Bryant Baylor!

"Ah!" I covered my eyes, but too late, my naked father-in-law's image was seared in my brain. I opened my eyes and looked somewhere else, but all I could see was a bunch of dangling tallywackers heading in my direction. "Don't come any closer," I said.

A splashing in the water redirected my attention. Ford was rushing out from under the waterfall. He saw me and swam fast in the direction of the shore.

Great, now he was going to think I was spying on him. Which I was, but I'd hoped I wouldn't get caught.

"Are you okay?" Bryant asked. "Do you need help?"

I kept my gaze level with the forty bare feet in front of me. "Nope. I'm good. Just go back to whatever you were doing, you know, before I...er...got lost in the woods."

"You're bleeding," Ford said when he got to me. He lifted me from the ground until I was standing, his body acting as a door between me and the rest of the shifters, many of whom I recognized, including one of my deputies.

"I'm fine." I touched my forehead where it stung and looked at my fingers. Yep. Blood. "Honest. I'm okay. I tripped on a stupid log and must have hit my head on something when I fell down."

"You're very graceful," he said.

I stared up into his gorgeous blue eyes, his dark hair dripped water over his chiseled cheeks. Goddess, he was handsome. I let my gazed wander down his glistening hairy chest to his thick, six-pack abs waist to the only log I really wanted to trip over.

When I looked back up to his face, his brows were raised. "In front of an audience? I had no idea you were such an exhibitionist, Hazel."

I smacked his chest, resisting the urge to caress. "I'm sorry," I said. "I just wanted to know what you were doing out here, and since you didn't volunteer the information..."

"I was sworn to secrecy," he told me and moved his eyes in a sideways direction to indicate the crew behind him.

"And you still are," Bryant said. Then he muttered something about crazy witches and other things I couldn't quite make out, then added, "But since she's here, you can give Hazel the basics."

"Where are you parked?" Ford asked.

I gave him a sheepish grin. "Just down the road here."

"How about if we get in my truck since it's closer and get you out of the cold? I'll just grab my clothes." Laughter sounded in the group of men. Ford grimaced. "Never mind. Apparently, my clothes have disappeared again."

"Is that why you've been coming home in ill-fitting clothing?"

He shook his head. "They are a bunch of children."

After he escorted me to the parking lot, Ford sat down next to me in the cab of his truck and put his arm around my shoulders. "I'm glad you're safe, babe. You had me worried when I heard you yell out. Why were you running through the woods?"

"Because I heard you roar like you were being mauled."

"Oh," he said, blushing. "The water in that water fall is pretty damn cold, add in the five-hundred-pound stone I had to hold over my head for the last twenty minutes while reciting Ursula's creed, well, you would have roared as well."

"Are you joining a fraternity? Go ahead, you can tell me. I won't judge you... much." I giggled.

"If this is what it's like to join a frat house then no thank you."

"They haven't paddled your bottom or anything, right? Because you can report that kind of thing nowadays." I caressed his scruffy jawline. "I'm sorry I made you worry. But I'm afraid I'll always make you worry. I don't want to watch you watch me die. You deserve better than three or four decades with someone. You deserve a lifetime."

"A lifetime without you is worse than death," he told me. "I am marrying you, Hazel Kinsey. The Goddess herself couldn't stop me."

"It's against shifter law to marry a human," I said.

"I've had enough rules, regulations, and rituals. I didn't just spend a month going through the Ursula Trials to not mate with you."

"Is that what it's called? The Ursula Trials? It sounds ominous?"

"It's a bear shifters rite of passage," Ford said. "This was the last one, thank the Goddess. These guys do not make it easy. It's tough and completely unnecessary, but I did it, because I want my entire clan to know that I'm devoted to you and them. I want them to take us both seriously when you become the *Arcturus*'s queen.

You are my mate, Haze. Witch or no witch. Scent or no scent."

Bryant Baylor knocked on the truck window on Ford's side. Thankfully, he was wearing pants now. When Ford rolled down the window, his dad said, "You're not alpha, yet, son. But I'm proud of you. You faced the trials with bravery and sheer will, and you endured. I bless the union between you and Hazel." He touched his forehead to Ford's. "I better get home. Your mom won't hold supper all night."

LATER THAT NIGHT, MY DAD AND TANYA CAME OVER TO check on me. Tanya said, "Ford called. He told us that you fell and hurt your head and scraped your hands. Do you want me to heal you?"

Her voice held a pity that made me cringe, but I nodded my head. Relief was relief. She put her hands on my shoulders again, mouthed her spell, and my minor wounds and new bruises healed.

"Thanks," I told her. I stood up and hugged my dad. "And thanks for sticking by me. You know, with the clowder. That took a lot of guts."

"There wasn't any other place I would have rather been."

Tizzy and Lupitia were curled up together on one of the couch cushions.

"At least we got Tiz back," I said.

"Damn straight," Dad replied. He hugged me tighter.

"Is this the line for the buffet?" my grandmother asked.

Tanya shot to attention. "Grand Inquisitor," she said. "How lovely to see you."

"Call me Clementine," my grandmother said. She cast an appraising gaze at my father. "Maybe one of these days, you will call me mother."

Tanya blushed and stammered as she cast a shy glance at my dad. "Maybe."

"Mom," my dad said through a tight smile. "This is an unexpected surprise."

"Isn't it, though?" She walked around the living room chairs and sat on the armrest of the sofa. "I hear you solved your familiar problem, Hazel. And you also solved another little problem for me, as well. You identified and dealt with Roberta Mendell's killers. Very efficient, but I wouldn't expect any less from my own flesh and blood. For that, I cancel the favors you owe me. We're even."

"Great." I liked being even. Even was way better than owing.

"I must say, though, I liked it when I had a favor banked." She breathed in deeply and chanted something that sounded like Latin.

The air around me grew thick and heavy. My head flung back as my lungs, of their own accord, expanded to inhale electrified air. I gasped when I was able to breathe again. "What was that?"

"I favor for a favor, my little witch."

I rubbed my fingertips together, feeling the spark of witchcraft under my skin. I grabbed a handful of my hair and looked at it. "No gray!" I danced up to my feet. My knees didn't give me any bit of trouble. And... I glanced down at my boobies. They were perky again. Yay! And I felt my bond with Tizzy once more. Even better. "But how? I thought you said you couldn't give me back my magic."

"No, I said I wouldn't interfere with the HFC. They are gone now and would have restored you if they could, so no interference on my part."

"But they said it would take all seven of them to reverse their curse."

She took on a scary omnipotent voice, and boomed the

words, "I am the Grand Inquisitor, queen of the witches, my power is all!"

"Really?"

"No, not really," she said in a normal voice. "But that was fun, huh? Seriously, though, I am pretty bad ass." She gave me a quick peck on the cheek. "Take care of yourself, my darling. And I expect an invite to that wedding of yours. Don't let it get lost in the mail." She nodded to my dad. "Stand up straight, Kent. You're slouching." And with that final observation, she apparated out of the room.

"That woman gives me the willies," Ford said.

"Yeah," I told him. "And now I owe her a favor again." I tried to sound unhappy about it, but I couldn't stop smiling. "You smell like fresh baked cinnamon crème cake," I whispered, his aromatic scent overwhelming my senses in the best possible way.

"And you smell like rum and cream soda." He nuzzled my neck and sighed happily.

I kissed his ear. "Take me to bed and bone me, baby. Let's bump uglies until my familiar learns to knock."

"Ewwww!" said just about everyone in the room.

I grinned. "Bite me. All of you." I grinned up at Ford.

"Shower first?" And with a snap of my fingers, I blinked Ford and I out of the living room and into…

Damn it! Wrong bathroom. I really needed to get better with my translocation spells.

Ford, who hadn't noticed, kissed me hotly. After he came up for air, he looked around, his expression ranging from confused to mortified. "Haze," he said. "How come we're in my dad's shower again?"

From the door, Bryant Baylor shouted, "Get a room, you two. Preferably one that isn't mine!"

I wiggled my brows at Ford and kissed his frowny pout. "Oops, my bad."

Ford chuckled. "There is never a dull moment with you, Hazel Kinsey."

I pinched his butt. "You bet your sweet cheeks," I told him.

The End

MURDER & THE MONEY PIT
BOOK 2

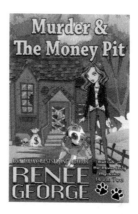

Shifter Lily Mason and her pit bull Smooshie are once again on the trail of a murderer and this time close to home!

Sometimes, trying to be part of the human world can be a real killer. . . Cougar-shifter Lily Mason is ready to put down roots in the human town of Moonrise, Missouri. She only has two problems: her attraction and proximity to Parker Knowles, her boss at the Pit Bull Rescue Shelter, and her need to shift into animal form more than once a month.

When she gets the opportunity to buy a "fixer-upper" outside of Moonrise with plenty of room to get wild without running into easily freaked-out humans, Lily jumps at the chance. Smooshie, Lily's lovable pit bull and partner in chaos, is eager to participate with the home improvements. Unfortunately, Smooshie's help includes digging out a mummified body from the living room wall.

Lily is still recovering from the last murder investigation she got involved in–and she's not looking forward to being in the middle of another one. The case gets even stickier when Lily's landlord is murdered, rumors of a heist gone wrong run rampant, and Parker's old high school buddies have returned to Moonrise, thus increasing the suspect pool. Lily's attempts to become a bona fide citizen of Moonrise might well be thwarted by this newest complication–especially when the murderer sets sights on her.

Murder & The Money Pit, Book 2 of the Barkside of the Moon Mysteries from USA Today bestselling paranormal cozy mystery author Renee George, is a gripping murder mystery that keeps you guessing from beginning to end!

Chapter One

I have never been an impulsive person. I look both ways before crossing the street, I test the water with my toe before wading in, and I don't buy dilapidated, two-story rural houses.

Oh, wait. Yes, I do. The decrepit home on twelve acres of wooded land outside Moonrise, Missouri, was mine-ish. I'd just signed an "as is" rent-to-own, fifteen-year contract with Merl Peterson, a property developer, and had given him a ten grand down payment.

What have you done, Lily Mason?

"The place needs a lot of work," Merl said. His bushy eyebrows were as thick and long as the hair on his head was thin and short. "It hasn't had any work done on it in a long time. I was planning to fix it up myself for a cushy resale price, but Greer's a hard man to say no to."

"Greer's a good man," I said. "One of the best."

Greer Knowles was a mechanic in Moonrise. He owned a small garage called The Rusty Wrench. He was the very first person I met when I came to town, thanks to my green and yellow mini-truck, aka the rust bucket. I've had the truck for over twenty years now, and Martha, even with her occasional problems, was still the most reliable thing in my life. At least, she'd been the most consistent. I looked over at her. Martha's wheel well rust had gotten worse over the winter. Salted roads had a tendency to speed up oxidation. But lucky for me, Greer knew how to keep her in top running order.

Greer was also the father of my boss and friend, Parker.

My heart picked up the pace, the way it always did when I thought of Parker. I was currently living over his garage in a small studio apartment. As much as I wanted independence and a place of my own, another reason this house was so important to me was because I needed distance from Parker.

It was hard working with a man I had feelings for when I knew nothing could ever come from them. Living right next to him made my heartache almost unbearable.

Merl pushed up his thick glasses and shook his head. "I have another place in town that's cheaper if this doesn't suit you."

What Merl didn't understand was that I liked the tall columns out on the porch and the ornate gables. There was something about this house, a certain charm, that I wanted to preserve. To make mine. Besides, my pit bull Smooshie needed room to run, to be free to stretch her thick legs. Frankly, I needed the same. As a werecougar living in a human town, I didn't often have the privacy needed to shift.

Smooshie barked and yipped with manic energy. I looked over in time to see my eighty-pound brown and white pittie leaping around after an orange and black Monarch butterfly near a patch of milkweed. We'd had a warm end to winter, and spring was a couple of weeks away. Even so, seeing a butterfly this early in March was unusual. Smooshie leaped again, her whole body twisting in the air.

I smiled. I really loved that dog.

"I'll be fine, Mr. Peterson. I have plans for the place."

"I hope a bulldozer's involved," he muttered.

I didn't say "what?" because I'd heard him loud and clear. My excellent hearing was the blessing and curse of being a cougar Shifter. I could also smell the remnants of his lunch— a burger with bacon, grilled onions, and bleu cheese. Buying a house on an empty stomach was no bueno. I turned to him and said, "Thank you, Mr. Peterson. I appreciate you taking a chance on me."

"Greer says you're okay, then you're okay in my book." The older man smiled, the lines around his eyes crinkling into small canyons. "Don't mind the ghosts." He grinned now.

Parker had tried to talk me out of the place. He'd said it was haunted. His expression had been so severe that I'd tried not to laugh. Not because I didn't believe in ghosts, quite the contrary. It's just that I grew up in a town with way scarier paranormal creatures than spirits. Besides, the ghost angle had allowed me to get the place at a steal. No one wanted to live in a house where people disappeared and were never seen from again. Except me.

"If it's all right, I'd like to hang out for a while, just to get some ideas and stuff," I told Merl.

"Sure," he said. "I'll have Jock Simmons send you copies of the contract. We'll get things finalized this week."

"It's okay that I get the trailer moved over and stuff now, right?"

"Of course. The place is yours. Just need to dot the i's and cross the t's, but as far as I'm concerned, you are home."

I smiled. "Sounds good." When Merl left, I pulled out my phone and made a call. "Haze. I got the house," I said when my BFF answered.

"Oh. Em. Gee!" She materialized and hugged me hard. "That's amazing."

Smooshie's barking grew even more excited, almost verging on a frantic hysteria as she danced around Hazel, going up on two feet, but not quite jumping on her.

"Will you muzzle your beast?" a squeaky voice demanded. A red squirrel climbed Haze to get away from my pittie.

"She's just saying hello, Tiz." I scratched Smooshie behind the ear, and she leaned her thick body into me, her tail whacking the back of my thighs as she panted her pleasure.

Hazel Kinsey is a witch, and Tizzy, a squirrel, is her familiar. They were both my best and only friends when I was growing up. Being short and skinny in a Shifter community was the same as being weak and useless. I'd never wanted to stay in Paradise Falls, but the death of my parents had made that choice for me. I'd had to drop out of high school to support my little brother, and I stayed until he died. It still hurt to think of Danny. There was nothing left for me there once he was gone.

"Is this it?" Tizzy asked. She made a chittering sound of disgust. "What a dump."

"Tiz!" Haze crossed her arms. "It just needs a little TLC. And maybe a little…" She wiggled her fingers.

"No magic," I said.

"Not even a little?"

"She's probably worried you'll blow her house down." Tizzy jumped to my shoulder. "Not that it would take much. Did you find this place in Deader Homes and Gardens?"

"Ha ha. Very funny."

"I thought so." Tizzy pulled an almond from somewhere on her furry person—I didn't want to know from where—and began to chew. "I like all the trees. And oh, look! Squirrels." Two gray squirrels ran up a mature maple. I rolled my eyes.

Haze, who was taller than me by six inches, put her arm around my shoulders. "You'll make it a real home, Lily. I have every faith."

"Thanks for lending me the down payment."

She smiled. "I know you're good for it." She gave me a squeeze.

"I'm kind of scared, Haze."

My BFF put her hands on my shoulders and stared down at me. "Why?"

"I'm not sure I can make it out here." By "out here" I meant in an entirely human town. Well, mostly. I'd never had to hide before, and I wasn't sure I could keep it up. "Aside from the fact that I'm a fish out of water—"

"More like a cat out of the litter box," Tizzy snarked.

I ignored her. "I didn't even finish high school. I don't make enough working at the shelter to afford a mortgage and food." Shifters burned through calories like fire burned through a month-old Christmas tree. And I needed a lot of protein in my diet, too. "Have you checked out the price of beef lately? It's ridiculous. I could spend a paycheck on red meat alone."

"Have you thought about getting your GED, maybe taking some classes at the local college?"

"I don't know."

"You're the smartest person I know, Lily Mason. It would be a shame to let all those brains go to waste."

Hazel believed every word she said. I could smell the truth on her. It was a gift passed down from my great-great-grandmother on my mother's side, who happened to be a witch, amazingly enough. I only found out in October that I wasn't pure Shifter, and some dangerous magic back home had triggered my ability as a truth-sayer. Most people wanted to be truthful, anyhow, and my power allowed them to open up to me. It didn't always work. If someone wanted to hide a secret bad enough, they could resist the compulsion to come clean.

I nodded to my friend. "I won't give up."

"Good, because you've been happy here, Lils. More happy than I'd ever seen you before." She squeezed my shoulders. "Humans are good for you."

"Yeah, yeah." I could hear the roar of a dually truck engine less than a mile away. "My boss is coming. You better get out of here."

"The boss?" She made *the* sound like *thee*. "The one who basically rescued you and swept you off your feet?"

"Stop," I said. "Seriously. You need to go."

Haze's phone played "Bear Necessities" from *The Jungle*

Book. "Shoot, that's Ford." She looked at the screen. "It's a 9-1-1. There's been trouble since Halloween between the Shifters and the witches, and with spring right around the corner, it's not getting any better." She kissed my cheek. "Call me if you need me."

"I'll be fine," I told her and gave her a quick hug.

"Bye, Lils!" Tizzy said as she circled her witch's waist and climbed up her back. "Next time leave your beast at home."

I knelt next to Smooshie, who happily wagged. "She is home."

Tizzy stuck her tiny tongue out at me. Haze gave me a wistful smile. "Tell lover boy I said hello."

"He's not—" They disappeared before I could finish my protest. Parker's big black truck was throwing dust up as it came down the gravel drive.

The truck ground to a halt about thirty feet away. Parker rubbed his hand over his dark hair before he opened the driver-side door and stepped out. He was average height, about five feet eleven inches, which was still eight inches taller than me. I'd always been a bit of a runt. He had a broad chest, muscular arms, and crystal-blue eyes that nearly undid me every time he looked my way.

His dog Elvis—half pit bull, half horse—jumped out of the truck after him. The large, silvery-blue beauty hugged his body against his master's legs. As a PTSD dog, Elvis had been trained to pick up on Parker's body language and put himself between Parker and stressors. Turns out I was one of those stressors. I didn't want to make Parker's life difficult. Just the opposite. It was the reason I needed my own place.

"Whatcha doing out here?" I asked, shielding my eyes from the sun as he approached. An easy breeze carried his scent to me, and I fought the urge to run into his arms. We were friends. Nothing more. No matter what my Shifter libido wanted.

"I have to run into Cape Girardeau for some supplies, and dad asked me to bring you out his toolbox, shovel, and plaster scraper." He reached into the bed of the truck and lifted out a red bifold-topped metal box.

"It's so I can bury the bodies."

Parker froze for a moment. A crooked smile played on his lips. "You need help? I got a hacksaw back home."

I laughed. "These will do." I took the shovel and scraper from him. I followed him to the porch where he set the toolbox down.

"There you go," Parker said. He rubbed his hands on his jeans and put them in the pockets of his windbreaker.

"Tell Greer I owe him some pie." It was a joke between us. Parker's dad and I shared a love of food in a pastry.

"I'll let him know." His low voice always made my stomach jittery.

Smooshie and Elvis sniffed each other, with Smooshie getting her full nose right up his butt. I didn't want to begrudge her the formal dog greeting of an old friend, but automatically, I said, "Stop that."

Smooshie cocked her head at me, gave Elvis one more nose goose then moved away. Thank heavens Elvis tolerated Smooshie. He outweighed her by at least thirty pounds.

"You sure you want to live out here?" Parker asked. "It's going to take a lot of work to get this place livable."

"Buzz is moving in with Nadine. He's going to let me put his trailer out here to live in until I can get it all fixed up."

Buzz was actually my uncle and was a good forty years older than me, but since we were both Shifters, we could pass for nearly the same age. Nadine was one of the few friends I'd made since I moved to Moonrise. She was a deputy sheriff for the county, and she was very much in love with my uncle. Unfortunately, she could never be Buzz's mate. Oh, he loved Nadine. He probably loved her as much as she loved him, but Buzz was a werecougar.

A Shifter. The only other nonhuman in town besides me.

Shifters only mated with other Shifters, with only a few exceptions, and all of those exceptions were paranormal mates. There was a distinct aroma that developed between mates, and when a Shifter caught the scent, it was for life. That couldn't happen in a Shifter-human relationship. It was genetically impossible. But since Buzz hadn't ever found his true mate, he and Nadine could be happy for many years together. Sadly, it would eventually end. And that was another reason to not get involved with sexy humans like Parker Knowles.

I felt an aching pain in my heart. My kind lived a very long time. Hundreds of years sometimes. I'm not sure anyone is built to watch the people they love grow old and die. I know I'm not.

"So Buzz is taking the big step, huh?" Parker smiled, his blue eyes lighting up with mischief. "He seems more like the rambling kind than the settling-down kind."

"Nadine has a way of getting what she wants." She reminded me a lot of Hazel. Nadine was very straightforward, a lot of "what you see is what you get." I admired her bluntness and her honesty.

I smiled at Parker; a melancholy feeling that I'd grown accustomed to experiencing washed over me. I knelt down, feeling the sudden need to hold on to something, in this case, my pittie. Smooshie put her wet nose to my ear and licked my cheek. I patted her.

"Theresa holding down the fort today?" I asked. She was Parker's other paid employee. He could only afford to have us both on part time thanks to an anonymous donation that rolled in every month on the fifth. Theresa Simmons, who had started as a volunteer, had worked at the Pit Bull Rescue Center for over two years. Parker also had several volunteers who spent time socializing the rescue dogs to get them ready for rehousing.

"Keith, Jerry, and Emily are in today, so she has plenty

of help."

"Good, I hated leaving you short on a Saturday. I know that's when you run your errands, but it was the only time Mr. Peterson had open to meet with me."

"Life happens." He glanced over at me, his blue eyes locking on my gaze. "They don't get much better than Merl Peterson. He gave me my first job, did you know that?"

"No, you never told me."

"Yeah, he likes to hire local teenagers for odd jobs. He'd hire me occasionally for things like deck building and roofing. Summer work. It was long hours but a decent paycheck."

"My first job I clerked at a convenience store. I worked nights and some weekends." I'd had to quit school to work full-time, and the Valhalla Gas & Go was the only place that would hire an eighteen-year-old dropout.

"I'm glad you're putting down roots here." He looked around, his upper lip curled a little in disgust. "Even if it's this place."

"The house has good bones," I told him.

"That's not a house."

"It has doors and windows and rooms and—"

"Ghosts."

"Parker."

"Facts are facts, Lily." He walked up the front steps as if

drawn, his voice like that of a tour guide. "Randall Dilley, who built the place back in 1908, hung himself in the living room. Another owner, Lincoln Edwards, was killed in a combine accident in the 1940s, a whole family disappeared from here in the eighties, and there hasn't been someone living there since Old Man Mills died in the upstairs bedroom two years ago."

"Let me guess." I mockingly gasped. "He was murdered."

"Nah. Natural causes." Parker paused. "Or so they say…" He let it hang there as if to imply there were more sinister reasons behind the old man's death. What he didn't realize is, because of my witch ancestor's gift, I could smell bull-poop from a mile away.

Anyway. I knew a little about John "Old Man" Mills. The property had been held in escrow as the court tried to find a blood relative somewhere to inherit. No one came forward, so the property was sold to Merl—who'd sold it to me.

"You want to go on the supply run with me?" Parker asked.

"No thanks." I smiled. "Another time. I want to get in and measure the rooms. I need to figure out where I want to start with this place. Besides, Buzz is bringing out the trailer today."

"That's fast." His lips thinned. "Well, thought I'd ask."

"And I appreciate it." To lighten the mood, I asked, "Do you think the ghosts took him out?"

"Who?"

"Old Man Mills, of course."

"I think he's one of the ghosts now." He moved in close, his tone ominous. "Some say when the moon is full, and the wind is right, you can smell his farts on the breeze."

I giggled. "That's terrible."

I will not flirt with Parker. I will not flirt with Parker. It had become my mantra. A mantra that failed fifty percent of the time.

I knew Parker liked me. A lot. I could scent his attraction. For whatever reason, his desire for me smelled like honey and mint. Crisp, refreshing, and exciting. But he deserved to be with a woman he could grow old with, and I had a terrible feeling that if I allowed myself to love Parker Knowles, I wouldn't be able to give him up when the time came for me to leave Moonrise. I could only stay for so long before people would start asking questions about why I didn't age, and the first rule of integrating with humans was to never let them know you were different. Not unless you wanted to be hunted down like an animal.

Humans had two impulses when it came to things they didn't understand. Kill it or dissect it. I didn't want either of those things happening to me.

One-Click "Murder & The Money Pit" To Read More!

CROSSOVER READING ORDER

- 1• Witchin' Impossible (Witchin' Impossible Cozy Mysteries Book 1)
- 2• Rogue Coven (Witchin' Impossible Cozy Mysteries Book 2)
- 3• Pit Perfect Murder (Barkside of the Moon Cozy Mysteries Book 1)
- 4• Murder & The Money Pit (Barkside of the Moon Cozy Mysteries Book 2)
- 5• Familiar Protocol (Witchin' Impossible Cozy Mysteries Book 3)
- 6• The Pit List Murder (Barkside of the Moon Cozy Mysteries Book 3)
- 7• Mr. & Mrs. Shift (Witchin' Impossible Cozy Mysteries Book 4)
- 8• Pit & Miss Murder (Barkside of the Moon Cozy Mysteries Book 4)

www.witchinimpossible.com
www.barksideofthemoonmysteries.com

PARANORMAL MYSTERIES & ROMANCES

BY RENEE GEORGE

Peculiar Mysteries

www.peculiarmysteries.com

You've Got Tail (Book 1) FREE Download

My Furry Valentine (Book 2)

Thank You For Not Shifting (Book 3)

My Hairy Halloween (Book 4)

In the Midnight Howl (Book 5)

My Peculiar Road Trip (Magic & Mayhem) (Book 6)

Furred Lines (Book7)

My Wolfy Wedding (Book 8)

Who Let The Wolves Out? (Book 9)

Madder Than Hell

www.madder-than-hell.com

Gone With The Minion (Book 1)

Devil On A Hot Tin Roof (Book 2)

A Street Car Named Demonic (Book 3)

ABOUT THE AUTHOR

I am a USA Today Bestselling author who writes paranormal mysteries and romances because I love all things whodunit, Otherworldly, and weird. Also, I wish my pittie, the adorable Kona Princess Warrior, and my beagle, Josie the Incontinent Princess, could talk. Or at least be more like Scooby-Doo and help me unmask villains at the haunted house up the street.

When I'm not writing about mystery-solving were-cougars or the adventures of a hapless psychic living among shapeshifters, I am preyed upon by stray kittens who end up living in my house because I can't say no to those sweet, furry faces. (Someone stop telling them where I live!)

I live in Mid-Missouri with my family and I spend my non-writing time doing really cool stuff...like watching TV and cleaning up dog poop.

Follow Me On Bookbub!

Printed in Great Britain
by Amazon